The Pony Trek

Gill Morrell

The Pony Trek

Published by PONY, Stabenfeldt A/S

Cover and inside illustration: Jennifer Bell

Cover layout: Stabenfeldt A/S

Typeset by Roberta Melzl

Edited by Marie Javins

Printed in Germany, 2005

ISBN: 1-933343-08-7

Stabenfeldt, Inc.
457 North Main Street
Danbury, CT 06811
www.pony.us

Chapter 1

"Jess! Phone for you!"

It took me a minute to stand up. I had to detach Tim, my baby brother, who was clinging to my legs like I was about to leave him forever, while simultaneously stopping his twin, Holly, from falling backwards onto the block tower we'd been carefully constructing. I love my brother and sister a lot, but taking care of them can be hard work. Over summer vacation and school breaks, I have to help Mom watch them.

I thought it'd be my best friend on the phone. It was the second to last week of summer vacation and we were trying to pack in as much fun as we could before school – and exams – hit us. But it wasn't Martha.

"Hi, Jess, it's Rosie. How are you?"

"Good. I've been keeping an eye on the twins all summer."

Rosie laughed. "That sounds like fun. Well, brace yourself. Are you sitting down? How does a week's riding starting on Sunday sound to you?"

"What!?"

"A week at the farm – well, not really at the farm – trail riding and camping with a gymkhana at the end. Whaddaya say? You up for it?"

I was speechless.

"Are you still there?" Rosie sounded worried.

"Yes," I managed to say. "But I don't get it. You know it's too

5

soon for us to afford another riding trip for me. Dad said maybe next Easter at the earliest."

"Yeah, I know, but that's the best part. Kate won't go, and it's too late to get a refund. Mom said I could ask you."

I thought rapidly. A week's free pony trekking would be fantastic, but I could see some problems.

"Look, Rosie, I'll have to talk to my parents and get back to you. When exactly would it be?"

"We're supposed to be at the farm on Sunday evening. Mom said you could ride with us if you can get to my house. It'd be so great. It's only for people who've been at the center before, and the first part of the week we go on a long pony trek, and camp out every night. We'll be by a lake, too, so we can swim. Then for the last couple of days we go back to the farm and do some training, and then we go to a horse show. This is the first year they've done it, and Kate and I booked as soon as we could. Didn't you get the details?"

As usual, I was embarrassed that my family had less money than Rosie's so I muttered something about having never gotten the letter. Actually, I remembered it perfectly well, but I hadn't looked at it because I knew there was no point and I didn't want to torment myself.

"Why can't Kate go? Is she sick?"

"Not really, but she's decided her arm hurts. I think she's lost her nerve."

That made sense. Kate, Rosie's older sister, had fallen off her pony right at the end of the pony vacation at Easter. She'd opened a gate without dismounting while her pony was overexcited. She'd broken her arm badly, but I knew it had been out of the cast for weeks now. Still, it had been a long summer without any contact with horses and she could easily have decided that riding was too risky.

I told Rosie I'd call her back as soon as I could, and then I sat on the stairs and thought. I could see several obstacles ahead.

First, Mom and Dad might say I couldn't accept a free vacation paid for by someone else.

Then, I'd have to get to Rosie's house in the city, which was miles from mine, or directly to the pony farm, which was equally complicated. Last time I'd taken a really long bus ride in both directions.

Last, we were going on a family vacation. Leaving Saturday. The twins, Mom and Dad and I. We'd all been looking forward to it all summer. How could I suddenly say I didn't want to go?

There was a squeal from the living room. Mom popped her head out from the kitchen.

"Jess, don't leave them alone. They could be up to anything..."

Sure enough, Tim was exploring the wastebasket, his fat diapered bottom stuck up in the air, while Holly was crying. It looked as if she'd tried to pull herself up and hit her head on the coffee table. I sighed, picked her up and cuddled her, hoisted Tim away from the trash by the straps of his overalls, and settled down with them by the blocks. They squeaked with excitement watching another tower grow taller and wobblier, while I decided to wait till after their bedtime to talk to Mom and Dad. This was going to need the right approach.

Predictably, the first thing Dad said, was, "No. Sorry, Jess, but we can't afford it."

"But, Dad, we wouldn't have to pay for anything."

"That's not very fair to Rosie's parents, is it?" said Mom.

"If I don't go, then they'll lose the money anyway. I told you."

"There's no need to be rude. What about our vacation? I thought you wanted to come with us."

"Well, yes," I squirmed with embarrassment. Of course, a week by the sea in an RV would be fun, even if the weather was likely to be dull and the twins infuriating. But compared with riding …

"Let me talk to Rosie's parents," Mom suggested. "I'm not promising anything, though."

Dad didn't look too pleased, but Mom was already dialing the number. She told me to go to my room so that she and Dad could talk. I hung over the banister as far as I could, but all I heard was the murmur of voices and later on, Dad sounding angry. Images of the farm kept flickering through my mind – the old stone house surrounded by fields, woods and marshes; Mr. and Mrs. Butler, who ran the center; all the friends I'd made there; and the ponies, Bramble and Poppy and Twinkle and Magpie; and the very best pony of all, my Tim, with his sturdy legs, soft gray coat and whiffly nose. Even his name was right – the same name as my baby brother. In my imagination, I could smell the scent of horses and fresh air and damp leather. I could hear the whinnies as Tim and Twinkle trotted over to Rosie and me early in the morning. The knot of excitement that had been growing inside me ever since Rosie's call felt ready to uncurl or burst.

"Come down, Jess," Dad called.

I skidded into the living room and looked at them anxiously. Dad looked annoyed and Mom had the strained look she gets when she's worried. My chances of going riding didn't look good.

"This isn't easy," Dad started. "We've all been looking forward to the vacation together. And your mother and I enjoy your company, strangely enough."

I decided this was a joke so I smiled tentatively. To my relief, Dad's expression lightened a little.

"On the other hand," he went on, "we understand how much you want to go on this trip. It does sound like a lot of fun."

"I'd learn a lot, too," I said breathlessly. Mom shook her head at me slightly and I shut up.

Dad went on, "Mr. Davies has insisted that we pay for nothing, and that they'd take you to the farm. It's a really generous offer. We've said you can go."

Time stood still while I reran that. Had Dad actually said yes or had I imagined it? Then I saw him grinning at me. I flung myself onto him and gave him a massive hug.

"There's one other thing," Mom added. "One of the reasons we've said yes is to thank you for being so helpful this summer with the twins. I couldn't have gotten by without you."

She hugged me too. With all that emotion going around, we'd probably have burst into tears if one of the twins hadn't started yelling.

"I'll go," I volunteered, and ran up the stairs. If being helpful got me to a riding vacation, then I'd keep on being helpful whenever I could.

This all happened on Wednesday, so there wasn't much time to get organized. At Easter, I'd worn cheap leggings, rubber boots,

8

T-shirts and sweatshirts. Most people had jodhpurs and riding boots, and I'd felt a bit silly at first, but no one seemed to mind. My big problem had been that the leggings had worn out quickly. Mom and I had a serious discussion about it, and she said she'd buy me some sweat pants that would be stronger. Everything else was still OK, but I thought I'd take shorts and a swimsuit in case the weather was good. After all, Rosie had said we'd be camping by a lake. The only other thing I had to take was a sleeping bag, and we already had that.

While all this was going on, I helped Mom get ready for the family vacation as well. On Saturday morning, we loaded the car with all the gear needed for a week away with one-year-old twins. They'd both picked up on the excitement and were being cranky, so I wasn't sorry I'd be traveling in the opposite direction very soon.

We went together as far as the bus station. I hadn't been there since the day I came back from my first pony vacation, when I'd been blown away by the fantastic time I'd had and couldn't wait to tell everyone about it. But I also remembered how terrified I'd been the Monday before, when I'd set off to a strange place, only too aware that I'd never actually touched a pony, let alone ridden one. This time I was happy, excited and just a little sad to be saying goodbye to Mom and Dad and the twins.

"I've got a surprise for you," Mom said as she gave me a hug. "We've decided to come to the farm on our way home and stay the last night nearby. We'll be there in time to watch this gymkhana you're going to be in and meet the ponies and everything."

"That'll be great!" I'd found it really strange describing everything about the farm to Mom and Dad when they'd never been there. Now they'd see me ride and understand just why I was so passionate about the place.

I kissed both twins' sweet-smelling, fluffy hair and gave Dad a quick hug. A few moments later, the bus swung out of the parking lot, bound not for the farm but for Rosie's house.

It was strange to see Rosie again. We'd met for the first time at the farm, spent a lot of time together there, and then had spoken once or twice over the summer. We'd planned to write or even meet up, but somehow there hadn't been time. I'd remembered her

9

14th birthday, though, and had sent her a card and a little china horse, and then she'd sent me a book about ponies for mine, a few weeks later. She was waiting at the bus terminal; her ginger hair was glowing in the sun and she looked really happy. He mother looked like Kate; slim, dark and pretty. She was friendly and welcoming and took us back to the car, and after half an hour we reached their house.

I knew Rosie and Kate had more money than us, but even so their house came as a shock – it was really big with an enormous yard. Rosie took me to her room. The walls were plastered with posters of pop stars and horses, and there were lots of pony books on her shelves. The little china pony I'd sent was on her bedside table.

We ate potato chips and discussed our plans for the week ahead. We didn't know too much about pony trekking, but it was fun to speculate. We spent a lot of time talking about the other people who'd been there at Easter, wondering if any of them might be on this trek.

"But since the center has different groups every week, it's unlikely that any others from Easter will be there," Rosie pointed out.

We talked about Kate, too.

"I don't think it's just the broken arm. I think she's just generally lost interest in ponies," Rosie said.

"Why?" I couldn't imagine anyone losing interest in ponies.

"Well, you know how she and Ed got together during the week?"

"Yes, but they split up, didn't they?"

"Oh yes, but it changed her. She's gotten really into clothes and makeup and going out with boys. I don't think there's time for ponies too. Maybe it'd be different if we had a pony of our own or could go riding every week. I've only had two riding lessons this summer. It's so hard to take lessons in the city. How 'bout you?"

I felt myself turn red. I didn't want to talk about my one encounter with ponies since the vacation. It was too embarrassing. But Rosie wouldn't let it drop, so I told her about it.

"Mom said I could have a lesson at a riding school a couple of weeks ago. I was really excited, well, you can imagine. But when I got there, it wasn't a bit like the farm. The ponies were different, too."

"What was yours like?"

"He was piebald – you know, black and white – and big, with heavy feet and hair all over them."

"Feathers," Rosie said knowledgeably.

"Yeah. And he wasn't friendly like Tim. He just looked bored."

"Go on."

"Everyone else knew each other and they were all younger than me. All their ponies were tiny, and then there was this huge clumsy pudgy one for me."

"That's kind of mean. It's horrible to be different."

"Exactly. Well, they were already tacked up, so we were told to mount, and I just couldn't get up on him. I mean, I'm not the greatest athlete in the world but I'm OK, but he was so tall. In the end I had to lead him over to a mounting block and everyone else laughed at me."

"But it's OK to use a mounting block."

"I know, but I was the only one…" I felt hot and flustered at the memory. "Anyway, then we went into an indoor school and walked around and around for ages. And the instructor kept yelling at me and telling me I was doing everything wrong."

"How mean!"

I shrugged. "Probably I was doing some things wrong, but the pony didn't take any notice of me anyway. You know how Mr. Butler tells us not to kick too hard? Well, if you didn't bash this one in the ribs, all he'd do is follow the others."

"Poor you," Rosie sympathized. "Did you do anything else but walk?"

"Oh yes. That's when it got worse. We had to trot a figure eight on our own. Everyone else could do it, and I couldn't get my pony to do it at all, and the instructor just sneered at me and asked if I had really been riding before because maybe I should be in a beginners' group."

"I'd have been furious."

"Well, yes, so was I, but that made things worse, because then I couldn't seem to concentrate at all. We did some cantering and then I fell off."

"You didn't get hurt, did you?"

"No, it was just that thing you and Kate told me about, being winded. It was horrible. I didn't think I'd ever be able to breathe again."

"And after that?"

"It was nearly the end of the hour, and I said I didn't want to get on the pony again. They said I had to. I didn't want to lose my nerve, so I mounted and just walked him around a bit, but you could tell he thought I was a total loser."

Rosie laughed. "How could you tell what the pony was thinking?"

"Just the way he looked at me. Kind of like, oh gosh, here we go again."

"So you didn't go back?"

"No, but to be honest I don't think Mom and Dad would have let me anyway. It was a long way from home, and it cost a ton. About the only good thing was that Mom didn't stay and watch, because I'd have died of embarrassment."

Rosie stood up and stretched. "Let's go out in the yard," she suggested. I followed her out and she took me down to where there was an ancient hammock strung up between two trees. We clambered in and sat precariously facing each other. It made me feel better after the unhappy memories I'd just been talking about.

"Tell me about your summer," I said.

Rosie described their family vacation and her two riding lessons.

"You're right that it seems strange being at a different place with different ponies," she said, "but to be honest the riding school ponies are generally better schooled than the farm ones. We did lots of jumping and I cleared a yard, and the second time we used the cross-country course and I did all the lower jumps OK."

"Did Kate go too?"

"The first time. She was looking forward to it, but when she got there she said she didn't feel well and her arm hurt, so she didn't ride. Last week she just said she had too much homework."

"It sounds like she really has lost her nerve," I said.

"Yeah, maybe you're right. You can imagine my parents weren't exactly pleased when she said she wouldn't come on the trek. Big fights. Lots of shouting."

I smiled sympathetically.

13

"Actually, it was Kate who thought of asking you. She thought Mom and Dad wouldn't mind as much if the money wasn't completely wasted."

I felt embarrassed and a little awkward. I'd imagined that Rosie had automatically wanted me to come. Rosie must have noticed because she stretched out her hand and squeezed mine.

"Don't worry, I'd have thought of you, too. Kate was the one in the thick of it. Anyway, it was a great idea, wasn't it?"

"Fantastic. I'm so excited. And grateful to your parents for inviting me."

It was Rosie's turn to redden, which made her freckles stand out oddly.

"Let's not talk about that. We did enough about your financial situation last time!"

I laughed. It was true; at Easter I'd gotten really neurotic about how little money I had compared to everyone else. Rosie had been supportive and cheerful and everything a friend should be. I made up my mind not to make a fuss about money all week.

There was the sound of running feet, and Kate appeared. She squeezed onto the hammock between us. She was friendly and chatty, and we talked about the Easter week and the people at camp all over again – though she kept off the subject of Ed. After a while, their mother called us for dinner. Rosie went ahead, so I took the chance to thank Kate for thinking of me.

"No prob," she said airily.

"You're sure you don't want to change your mind?"

"Me? No, I've got loads to do this week. History homework and studying for a physics test on the second day of the semester."

"And a boyfriend?" I said, hoping to cheer her up.

"Yeah, well, sort of. On and off, you know. Anyway, say hi to the ponies for me, especially Magpie."

"Sure," I said, remembering Magpie, who was black and white like the pony I'd recently failed to ride, but a lot nicer. "Maybe you'll feel like coming again next year."

"Who knows? Look, this is where we eat."

She showed me to the big living room with a table at one end. Their Dad had come home from work, so I had to say hello and

14

thank him, and there wasn't time to talk to Kate again. I felt sorry for her, though. It seemed to me that it wasn't work or boyfriends keeping her away from ponies; just the thought of another bad fall. But on the other hand, there wasn't much I could do about it, so I might as well enjoy the opportunity I'd gotten. I put Kate's problems in the back of my mind, ate lasagna and salad, and chatted with her family. I went to bed later full of excitement tinged with just the faintest of worries that the instructor might have been right and I might really and truly have forgotten how to ride.

Chapter Two

We got to the farm in time to visit the ponies before dinner. It was a beautiful evening. The sun was shining. There was the gentlest of breezes to lift the heat, and there was that amazing scent of horses and fresh air that I'd tried to recapture all summer but had never really been able to remember perfectly.

Mrs. Butler was waiting for us, and told us we'd be in the same bedroom as before, when we'd shared with Kate. We said a quick goodbye to Rosie's Mom, ran upstairs and dropped off our bags, and then came down and looked into the big common room. No one was there – they were either outside or hadn't arrived yet. It was strange being back, and seeing the squashy sofas and the shelves full of books and model horses. So much had happened here.

We found Mrs. Butler in the kitchen as usual. She handed us each an apple. We perched on the table and asked her about the other riders.

"There aren't as many of you as usual," she said, as she stirred a big pot of stew.

"Isn't the pony trek popular?" asked Rosie. "I'd have thought lots of people would want to come."

"No, we limited it to eight because so many of the ponies need a break," Mrs. Butler said.

"Not Tim?" I asked anxiously.

Mrs. Butler thought for a moment. She didn't really deal with the pony side of things.

"No, Tim's fine," she said at last.

Relieved, I did a quick mental count. "There were twelve of us last time," I said.

"That's right. That's our maximum, usually. But camping's different."

"Are you coming with us?" asked Rosie, throwing her apple core towards the trashcan and missing. "Oops." She jumped down and went over to put the core in properly.

Mrs. Butler laughed. "Me? Have you ever seen me riding?"

"No, but you do, don't you?" I asked. I couldn't imagine anyone lucky enough to live in such a beautiful place – and surrounded by ponies – choosing not to ride.

"I used to, but I've given up now. Getting too old. And even if I did ride, I wouldn't want to go camping. It's far too uncomfortable for me. I'll stay here and keep an eye on things while you're away with Dave and Caroline."

Dave was Mr. Butler who ran the center. He could be kind of scary, but he'd been helpful when I had no idea how to ride. His assistant, Caroline, was only about 20. She was kind, but had absolutely no control over us, so I suppose he did have to be the strict one.

Rosie was looking out of the kitchen window into the stable yard. "You'll never guess who I've just seen," she said suddenly.

"Who?"

"Guess."

"Brad Pitt?" I said sarcastically.

"No, silly. Someone from Easter time."

My stomach did a little wiggle. "Mike?" I said.

You could say that Mike and I had a difficult relationship. He'd gotten angry with me at the start of the week when I'd helped another boy that he was teasing. Then, as revenge, he'd decided to bully me. He'd loosened Tim's girth so I'd fallen off disgracefully, he'd hit me "by mistake" with a riding crop, and worst of all he'd pushed me into a stinking heap of manure. But with a little help from Rosie, I'd stood up to him, and at the end of the week we'd made up and even seemed to be friends. I wasn't sure I wanted to spend a whole week with him again, though.

"Not Mike. Guess again."

"Rosie! I could be here till midnight!"

"Hardly," put in Mrs. Butler. "There were only twelve of you, after all. Who is it, Rosie? I can't remember now who else was on your vacation. We've had so many groups through here since."

"Phil," announced Rosie.

She smirked at me. I knew what she was thinking. Phil had liked me a little, and though I didn't like him that much, he was around a lot, and he'd actually given me his phone number the last evening. In a stupid moment I'd told Rosie that, and now she'd been imagining all sorts of things.

"Oh yes, of course, it was the really dramatic week when your sister broke her arm," remembered Mrs. Butler. "Well, I just hope that Phil's gotten a bit more sensible about food since Easter."

Rosie and I exchanged smiles. Phil was the pickiest eater I'd ever met, and he complained at every meal – which must have been really irritating for Mrs. Butler. She was a fantastic cook.

"Let's go outside and see where everyone is," I suggested.

"Poor Jess, Phil's gone into the cabin," Rosie teased as we went through the hall and out into the sunny yard. The cabin was next to the house and was where all the boys slept. It was out of bounds for us girls, just as the second floor of the house was out of bounds for them.

I decided not to rise to Rosie's bait so I pretended not to have heard. Anyway, there were far too many other things to do. The ponies lived in a large paddock beyond the tack room, where all the saddles and bridles and cleaning equipment were kept. We leaned on the fence as we'd often done before and looked at the grazing ponies. I saw my Tim right away. He was easily the prettiest of all the ponies at the riding center, with his almost-white coat and his flowing mane and tail. I remembered how long it had taken to get them silky and tangle-free every day, and hoped his summer riders had taken care of him as well as I had. I chirruped in the special way I'd invented at Easter. He lifted his head from the short grass almost instantly and looked at me. I was really thrilled when he came trotting over and thrust his soft nose over the fence into my outstretched hand.

"He remembers me!" I felt so privileged to have such a perfect pony.

Meanwhile, Rosie had climbed the fence and gone over to Twinkle, who she'd ridden on several vacations. Twinkle was a chestnut, with a graceful neck and gentle manners. She was also a lot sturdier than Tim, which was probably a good idea for Rosie, who wasn't very tall but wasn't exactly thin either. The other ponies wandered over curiously, and Rosie disappeared into a sea of gray, brown and black. I could hear her talking to all of them. I was happy to stay with Tim. I liked the other ponies, of course, but Tim was special. He'd taught me how to ride. He'd been endlessly patient as I tugged his mane and pulled at his mouth the first few days, never complaining when I put his tack on wrong or gave him the wrong cues.

A bell rang from the house, which meant dinner was ready. Rosie emerged from the gaggle of ponies, while I gave Tim a hug and kissed his soft cheek.

"See you later," I said. We went indoors.

The common room had filled in our absence. Rosie and I stood in the doorway and looked around at a group of girls and one boy. Then Rosie squealed, "Emily!" and flung herself on a girl I'd never seen before. I couldn't see Phil and there wasn't anyone I knew, so I just stood there feeling silly. Then Rosie dragged Emily over and introduced us.

Emily was dark like me, but really skinny. She was wearing jeans and a tank top, which showed off her bony shoulders. She stared at me in the most hostile way you can imagine.

"Emily and I shared a room last summer," Rosie explained in an excited voice. "We were such good friends, but we haven't met up since. Em, this is Jess who I shared with at Easter."

How was it that Rosie made me feel like I was the substitute, second best after the amazing Em? I vaguely remembered hearing about her before, but I hadn't had the impression that they'd been inseparable or anything. Emily and Rosie pushed past me to go to the kitchen and danced back almost at once.

"Em's moving in with us. Isn't that great?" announced Rosie.

"Great," I agreed politely. I'd sat down at one end of a sofa, next

to a pretty black girl who was busy talking to someone else. But now she turned to me and said hello.

"I'm Jess," I said.

"Megan," she replied. "Is that your sister?" She looked at Rosie.

"No, she's a friend. We met here at Easter, so we've come back together. Have you been here before?"

As I said that, I remembered that everyone had to have been to the center before, but Megan didn't seem to think I'd said anything silly. She explained that she'd been twice; both last year and the year before.

"Did you come on your own each time?" I asked.

"Not the first time. It was a school trip; we had an activity week at the end of seventh grade, so we all knew each other. Most of us couldn't ride at all, so it was a slow week! I don't think we even trotted until Wednesday."

"Did you come back with school last year too?

"No, I was with a friend. She's not here this time, though. She's in Florida doing Disney."

"Lucky her," I said.

"Um, but I think I'd rather be riding for a week. How about you?"

I explained a bit about how I'd come alone, a complete beginner, at Easter. I told Megan that Rosie had suggested we come back together, but I didn't mention about Kate dropping out at the last minute.

Mrs. Butler announced supper. Rosie squeezed my arm affectionately as we went through to the dining room.

"It'll be such fun for the three of us," she said. "You'll love Em; she's a real laugh. Isn't it nice of Mrs. Butler to move her in with us?"

"Great," I said unenthusiastically, sitting down.

"Hi, Jess." It was Phil, sitting down next to me and looking really pleased to see me. We exchanged news about the summer and our families. Phil was an only child. The first time we'd met, he gotten really upset with me because I'd said I was too – sort of forgetting-on-purpose about the twins – and then I'd had to admit to them. He'd also made a terrible fuss about not liking the food every time we'd had a meal, and then later he'd gotten hungry and eaten all my cookies. On the other hand, he was kind and he'd helped me a lot when I didn't know what I was doing around the ponies. And he was quite good-looking, which always helps – tall with curly brown hair and such a nice smile.

"Are any of the others from your school here?" I asked.

"Not this time, no."

The stew and baked potatoes were being served so we didn't say anymore for a while, and then afterwards there wasn't time to chat. Mr. Butler gathered everyone in the common room and went over all the details of the week.

"We're going to trek over the next three days, camping out at night, cooking our own food and making our own entertainment," he explained. "So look carefully at the kit list and check that you've got everything you need. There won't be any shopping opportunities on the way."

"Oops, sorry. I've just realized that I forgot my sleeping bag," said the other boy. He had dark brown hair and a mischievous grin and generally looked gorgeous.

"Tom, you're a nightmare," said Mr. Butler, although it looked to me as if he had a soft spot for Tom. "Every time you come, you forget something. One of these days, I'll find you riding without a pony."

Everyone laughed.

"Lucky for you, we've got a spare sleeping bag," said Mrs. Butler, "though it'll probably turn out to be one that you left here last time."

"Next, the ceremonial handing-in of the cell phones," Mr. Butler announced.

There was a general groan.

"Do we have to?" asked one of the girls I hadn't met yet. Her voice was so elegant. "How can we keep in touch with our friends?"

"Sorry, Camilla, it's a house rule," said Mr. Butler firmly. "No exceptions. Your parents can contact us in an emergency, but other than that we'll have a cell-free zone for the week. Hand them over."

He passed around a bag and everyone, including me, put in a phone. I'd finally persuaded Dad and Mom that I had to have a cell phone, and they'd given me one for my birthday. I didn't mind not using it for a few days. I'd look stupid riding along with a phone stuck to one ear.

Camilla sighed heavily as she put her top-of-the-range model into the bag. I suddenly noticed that the girl next to her looked almost identical. They must be twins. The twin turned red as she put her phone into the bag. I vaguely wondered why, but we moved on quickly.

"You'll need to have your kit ready to be packed into saddle-bags after breakfast," said Mr. Butler. "Then we'll catch the ponies and get them groomed and saddled up. I'd like to be off by eleven, so breakfast is at 8.30 and then straight to work. Any questions?"

"What do we do for showers while we're away?" asked Camilla.

I'd wondered about that. Rosie and I had discussed it in the car and her Mom had said the camps would probably be near farm-houses so we could use the facilities there.

"No showers," Mr. Butler said firmly. There was a sort-of communal gasp as we girls reacted to this.

"We can't not shower!" said Emily.

"Maybe there are bathtubs instead?" suggested Camilla's twin hopefully.

"What, canvas ones carried around on a pony's back?" answered Mr. Butler, looking as if he wanted to laugh. "We're not going on a luxury safari, Georgie."

"But how do we keep clean?" asked Camilla.

"Dear oh dear," said Mr. Butler. "You girls get worse every year. First it's the phones, now this. Let me explain. We're going on a pony trek. We're going into the middle of nowhere. We're camping in the wild. How could there be showers and toilets out there?"

This time the gasp was even louder. No toilets? I'd been to fairly primitive camping sites with Mom and Dad, so I wasn't too surprised that there might not be showers, but toilets! Someone said, shakily, "How do we go to the bathroom, then?"

"You dig a hole, with a little shovel," said Mr. Butler, firmly. There was a long silence, broken by someone saying, "Yuck!"

"And if the weather's OK, you can swim in the lake on Tuesday."

There was another horrified silence, broken by Tom.

"Cheer up, girls," he said. "You'll survive. The ponies won't care if you don't smell as sweet as usual."

"It's not us we're worried about," retorted Megan quickly. "It's you boys stinking of BO."

"What nerve! I'll bet you that we stay at least as clean as you bunch."

"Oh, yeah?"

"OK, OK, that's enough," broke in Mr. Butler. "Why don't you all work on the principle that you won't smell? You're going to have water; there's nothing to stop you from washing. Come on now, it's getting late and there are a few more things we need to talk about."

The meeting went on for another hour. Afterwards, he sent us straight up to bed, saying it would be an exhausting week and we'd need our sleep. The boys went off to the cabin and we girls gathered outside the two bathrooms upstairs to work out a schedule, so we'd all get time to have a bath or shower before breakfast.

There were six of us in all: Rosie, Emily, Megan, the twins Camilla and Georgie, and me.

"When did you all come here before?" asked Georgie. We all explained.

"We've been twice," she said. "Once last summer and once this past summer. I suppose you all ride at home?"

"I don't," I said quickly. I wanted it to be quite clear that no one should expect me to be a great rider.

"Me neither," said Megan. "Just the two trips here and a little on other vacations with my family."

Rosie had a bit more experience. Emily said that she went riding every week and had been to the center once before, when she'd met Rosie.

"And what about you two?" she asked.

"We've been riding for years," said Camilla. "But we're not allowed to have our own ponies because of school."

"Too much homework?" asked Megan, sympathetically.

"No, we're at boarding school. We wouldn't see the ponies for weeks at a time, so we have to use riding school ones instead. It's such a pain. Most of our friends have their own ponies."

"You poor things," said Megan. I looked at her and realized she was being sarcastic and thought about how much I liked her. The twins, on the other hand, obviously thought she was being completely genuine and agreed that they were deprived. How the other half live, I thought. If they only knew how Mom and Dad needed to scrimp and save for me to do any riding at all; how I wasn't even paying to be here… I decided I wasn't going to like the twins. They were far too snobbish and rich for me. But Megan seemed fun, and Rosie would be around – when I could detach her from Emily, who was being very clingy, whispering to Rosie a lot and making it look like they had private jokes – and then there'd be Phil, and Tom – who looked as if he'd be a real asset to the group.

"I'm going to bed," I said. "It doesn't sound as if we'll be exactly sleeping in comfort for the next few days, so we'd better get what we can now."

We all said good night and went to our rooms. Megan was alone now that Emily had moved in with us. I hoped she didn't mind. I didn't exactly want to suggest I move to her room, though – Rosie was my friend and I didn't want to alienate her.

We got undressed and lay in bed chatting lazily. Emily was full of stories of her extremely boring family and the exploits of her tedious dog. Why on earth would we be interested in how some overfed Labrador behaved? I dropped out of the conversation and pretended to be asleep. A picture of my darling Tim swam into my mind; I could almost feel his velvet muzzle and the texture of his long mane. Caressing his strong, soft neck in my imagination, I drifted off into real sleep.

Chapter Three

Our roster didn't work too well the next morning. I was supposed to be third in line for the shower room, but Emily decided she'd prefer a shower to a bath and then took forever, but didn't tell anyone. I was waiting for the shower and wondering why Megan was taking so long when actually she'd finished long before. By then it was too late for me to swap and have a bath instead, and I ended up standing under a lukewarm shower before rushing down to breakfast – still damp and feeling cross and disorganized.

"Ah, Jess, still turning up late for breakfast, I see," said Mrs. Butler brightly.

I blushed. At Easter I'd been late once or twice, and the reputation had somehow stuck.

"It wasn't my fault," I started, but Mrs. Butler shushed me and told me to eat.

She'd cooked a massive amount of bacon, sausage and scrambled eggs.

"To keep you going over the next three days," she said

"Does that mean we're going to starve?" whispered Rosie to me. She was being friendly this morning, so I felt better about her.

"Maybe we have to catch our own food while we're away?" I murmured back.

"What, fishing and things?"

"Um, or mushrooms and berries."

We looked at each other in a moment of mutual horror.

26

"Let's eat now," said Rosie, and she wolfed down mouthfuls of hot food before buttering several slices of toast.

I couldn't manage so much. I was actually feeling nervous about riding and whether I'd remember what to do. I knew Tim would help me and that it would be nothing like the horrible experience I'd had at the riding school. All the same, I rubbed my stomach as the memory of the agony of that fall came back to me. I wished fervently that whatever happened this week, I wouldn't get winded again.

I was dying to see the ponies, but we had to get our stuff packed into saddlebags first. The bags were tricky. I looked at the pile on my bed and realized that there was no way it would all fit in.

"This is impossible!" Emily wailed. She'd pushed everything she could into her bags but the pile left still looked as big as mine. She pulled everything out and we all looked at the packing in despair.

"Let's have another look at Mr. Butler's list," suggested Rosie, who had a lot of common sense except where friends and sisters were concerned. "I'll read it out loud and we'll each put that thing in and we'll see what happens."

She started reading and packing, and we did the same. Amazingly, by the end there was still a little space in our bags – but the number of items still on the beds was horrific, and most of them were necessities.

"Makeup," said Rosie. "I'm not going anywhere without my makeup bag."

We all agreed and stuffed the bags in.

"I can't manage with just one sweater," said Emily. "The one I've put in doesn't match my spare T-shirt. I'll take this red hooded sweatshirt. And I need a pair of jeans for the evening."

"You'll never get it all in," warned Rosie. She was right. Emily threw the clothes back on the bed angrily.

"What about books?" I said.

"Will we have time to read?"

"Who'd want to take a book?" said Emily, as if I'd said something weird.

Obviously not you, I thought. Out loud I said, "Well, I'm going to put one in, just in case."

Rosie was squashing everything to one side in order to squeeze in a long thin box. I caught a glimpse of the writing on it.

"Rosie! You don't need your hair straighteners! And anyway, there won't be any electricity."

Rosie looked stubborn. "Maybe not, but I bet I'll find somewhere with electricity at least once a day. I'm not going back to frizz."

I looked at Rosie's hair. It had gotten a lot straighter since Easter, though to be honest I hadn't noticed before.

When no one was looking, I pushed in a little teddy bear – the one I take with me everywhere – and a spare T-shirt. Meanwhile, Emily was struggling with bottles of shower gel, shampoo and conditioner.

We finished packing at last, though there were still things left over, especially spare clothes. All we were meant to take was underwear, a sweater, a pair of shorts, rainwear, a swimsuit and a towel. The bags weighed a ton, but that would be for the ponies, not us. I felt sorry for Tim, but I comforted myself with the fact that I was much lighter than Rosie.

Downstairs, everyone was milling about while talking loudly and excitedly. A pile of sleeping bags and nylon bags containing the tents lay in the middle of the floor. Caroline staggered in from the kitchen with a saddlebag stuffed full of food and another that looked quite odd with frying pan handles sticking out.

"Oh good, we don't have to find our own food after all," murmured Rosie to me.

"Unless that's just Caroline's supplies," I whispered back. Caroline was extremely large; I couldn't imagine her surviving on anything but three square meals a day. Micky, her skewbald pony was equally solid and plonked along cheerfully on feathered hoofs that made him look like a slightly short carthorse, completely different from Mr. Butler's beautiful but snooty Captain, who always seemed to be looking down his nose at the ponies.

"Hi, everyone," she said with a big grin. "Right, don't remind me. Let's see how many of you I can remember."

Considering how many riders came to the center week after week, she was amazing at identifying most of us from the list in her hand. She even remembered that I'd been a complete beginner, and said something nice to me about learning even more this time. Then she told us to carry our bags out to the yard.

Weighed down, we staggered out into the open air. It was so cool to be back in the countryside. It was so quiet; you felt as if you could hear sounds from ten miles away. It was warm, too. Somehow I'd forgotten that it wouldn't be exactly the same as at Easter, when the weather had been OK but not especially hot. Now, in August, the sun shone from a cloudless sky and the breeze was just enough to lift the heat.

"Let's hope this lasts," said Rosie, next to me. "Wouldn't it be great to spend a whole week outdoors in this?"

"I don't care even if it does rain," I said. "So long as we're riding."

"Make sure you use lots of sunscreen," Phil warned. He was rubbing lotion onto his face and neck.

Rosie sighed. "You'd be a much nicer person if you stopped fussing," she said.

Phil looked hurt. "I'm not fussing, just using common sense. You can get sick."

"I know, I know. Just don't fuss."

Phil went off on his own and I giggled. It was so good to be back with Rosie and to hear her straightforward comments. She never took any nonsense from anyone.

We were all standing around instead of going to fetch our ponies as we usually would, because Caroline had told us to wait while they checked on who got which pony. But I knew I'd be riding Tim because at Easter I'd asked and they'd said I could, so I wandered into the tack room and had a look at Tim's tack – his saddle and bridle. I inspected them carefully to see if they were as clean as when I'd left them. The leather saddle gleamed warmly but the iron stirrups were a little muddy. I put my saddle-bags down under the hook and found a cloth to wipe the mud away. I lifted down the complicated web of leather straps, metal bit, and jangly rings that magically fitted over Tim's head to become a bridle, and ran my fingers along the reins. They felt just as I'd remembered – pliable, comfortable, and natural. It almost felt as if I was already riding …

"Jessica!"

I whizzed out into the yard to find everyone gathered around Mr. Butler. They were all looking at me.

"Sorry," I said.

"Pay attention, Jess. It's a complex business getting you all ready for a three-day trek. If you miss something vital, you'll only be sorry later."

"Yes, Mr. Butler."

It felt just like school, except that at school everyone around you is a friend, or at least someone you know. Except for Rosie and Phil, everyone here was still more or less a stranger. They all looked frighteningly efficient and well dressed, too. At Easter, I had gotten insecure about being the only one without real jodhpurs, and almost the only one without riding boots. Looking around, it looked like this was going to be a rerun. My sweat pants were comfortable, but they didn't look at all like jodhpurs, unlike the old leggings, and my rubber boots were the only ones this time. I was positive everyone was noticing how badly I was dressed, especially the twins, who looked as if their outfits were ready for a fashion spread – pale jodhpurs, cream shirts, and dark blue fitted jackets. In fact, Mr. Butler commented on that almost as I thought it.

"Georgie, Camilla, what you've got on'll be great for the last day when we go to the horse show, but we're going camping. Don't you have any older clothes?"

"Not really. No," said Camilla.

"We could leave our jackets behind if you'd like," offered Georgie. "But the list said we needed something in case it rained."

"I was thinking more of a raincoat," said Mr. Butler. "But I suppose there's no reason why you can't wear those. Just don't get them too filthy. I don't want your parents to complain."

"These are our old things," remarked Camilla in an offhand way. "We've got better clothes for Saturday."

There was a silence. I looked around. Everyone else was wearing ordinary jodhpurs and either boots or shorter pony boots, and T-shirts. At least I'd got that right.

"Suit yourselves," said Mr. Butler, shrugging. "OK everyone, ponies."

The center had fourteen ponies. On my last vacation, twelve of them had been in use, plus Captain and Micky. This time there were only eight of us, but one extra pony would be needed to carry the tents and cooking things.

"Poppy's lame," Mr. Butler announced, "and anyway, she's a bit small for any of you."

Poppy had been one of my favorites last time. She was tiny but brave, and very quick. But it was true that we were all quite big this time; in fact, I was probably the lightest, though Rosie was shorter than I.

"And Meg and Arthur need a rest. They've been working non-stop."

Meg was neat and pretty and had been Jane's pony before. I was sorry she wouldn't be in use. I'd have liked a chance to ride her. I didn't remember Arthur, so he must have been having Easter week off.

"So that leaves us with Bilbo, Twinkle, Bramble, Star, Rolo, Tim, Magpie, Mr. Man and Campbell. Campbell will be the pack pony as he's strong and good at being led."

"Who had Campbell last time?" whispered Rosie.

"Rob. Don't you remember? He's almost black with a brown tail."

"Who – Rob or the pony?"

"The pony, silly."

"Of course. I wonder which I'll get. I wouldn't mind Mr. Man this time."

I looked at Rosie in amazement. Surely she'd want to ride Twinkle again? But there was no time to think. Mr. Butler was reading out the list.

"Ladies first. Emily – Mr. Man. Camilla – Magpie. Rosie – Twinkle. Megan – Star."

"Brilliant, the best pony!" exulted Megan.

"I'm glad you think so. Jess – Bilbo. Georgie – Tim. Then for the boys, Phil – Bramble and Tom – Rolo."

I stood dumbfounded. I'm sure my mouth was hanging wide open. Then I gathered my senses and said, "'I think there was a mistake. You got me and Georgie confused."

31

Mr. Butler glanced down at his list. "Georgie's got Tim and you're riding Bilbo. Oh, sorry Jess, did you want Tim again? We can't always manage that, not if two of you have had the same pony before."

"But you said I could …"

"We do try, Jess. We can't manufacture two ponies out of one. You didn't book till pretty late, did you? The twins booked ages ago."

I looked straight at Georgie, willing her to be generous and give Tim up to me, but I had no such luck. She just shrugged, flicked back her blonde hair and looked at me coolly with her very blue eyes.

"You're not the only one who's got a different pony," said Caroline, putting an arm comfortingly around my shoulders. "Emily's never ridden Mr. Man before, and Tom had Bramble last time and now he's got Rolo."

"Yes, but..." I couldn't carry on. I was ready to burst into tears and then everyone would think I was stupid. I pulled myself together and muttered something. I pretended I'd left something inside, and by the time I came back out everyone seemed to have forgotten about me.

They were collecting the ponies from the paddock. That's not as easy as you'd think. The ponies all wore head collars made of rope so that there was something to grab hold of, but it all depended on whether they wanted to be caught in the first place. I'd never had any trouble with Tim, who was totally sweet natured and had always trotted straight over to me when I'd made the special chirruping sound. To my irritation, he was doing exactly the same thing for Georgie, though she was just saying "Tim, Timmy" in a rather silly way.

I identified Bilbo in the center of a group of ponies at the far end of the paddock. He had been Mike's pony, and I'd started off badly with him as he'd bitten Tim. The last day, Mike and I had been paired for a treasure hunt, and I'd had more to do with Bilbo, but I hadn't gotten to know him very well. He was black, with a short, spiky mane, and thin – very different from Tim.

"Cheer up," said Rosie. She came by leading Twinkle, looking

32

happy. It was all very well for her; she'd gotten the same pony and she didn't even care.

I ignored her and trailed over to the ponies. Some of the other riders passed me with their ponies. Georgie was already putting Tim's tack on, back in the stable yard. By the time I reached the bottom of the field, there was only Camilla and Tom left. Magpie was being frisky, pretending to come to Camilla and then jumping away. She got out a piece of sugar and held it out on her open palm. Magpie sidled up, extended his elegant nose to her hand, and while he nuzzled the sugar she had her hand on the rope and leapt impressively onto his bare back and trotted him up to the yard.

Meanwhile, Tom had grabbed Rolo, who was a big, heavy gray pony. That only left Bilbo loose. I put out an arm feebly and chirruped like I used to do to Tim, but Bilbo ignored me. Instead, he took a casual nip at Rolo as the bigger pony went by. Bilbo then cantered over to the far side of the field.

"Sorry," I said to Tom, who'd managed to hold on to Rolo even though he'd skittered with surprise.

"Don't be," he replied. "I know Bilbo from before. I had him the first time I came here and he nipped me twice. But he's all right, you know; just a bit bold. Can you catch him OK?"

"Thanks. I'll be fine."

"Well, have some carrot. It works wonders."

He passed me a chunk of carrot and led Rolo away.

Holding the carrot and still chirruping hopefully – and feeling very silly – I pursued Bilbo around the field. It took me ten minutes to catch him, by which time most people had their ponies tied to the fence and were busy tacking up, except when they were watching me make a fool of myself. When I finally led Bilbo up, the rope stretched to full length as he followed me unenthusiastically. I was feeling a lot less excited about this pony trek than I'd been before.

I tied Bilbo to the paddock fence, well away from the other ponies. I didn't feel like getting into trouble for letting him nip anyone. While I was in the tack room, I found a riding hat. It was the same one I'd had before, but it felt strange. I'd forgotten how rigid it felt, how awkward the chinstrap was, balanced right on the point of your chin rather than under it; even how heavy it was.

33

Camilla came in while I was adjusting the straps. Of course, there was no question of her borrowing a hat. Hers was navy blue velvet and looked as if it was brand new.

"You're not actually supposed to share riding hats," she remarked.

"Why not?" Had the farm changed its policy since Easter and not told me about it?

"It's so not safe. We had a talk about it at school."

"At school!" I echoed. What sort of school gave lessons about riding? My school barely acknowledged that horses exist.

Camilla shrugged. This seemed to be both twins' reaction to anything they considered strange. "I wouldn't fall off if I were you," she warned. She picked up a leading rein and left.

Feeling kind of uncertain, I finished adjusting the hat. If what Camilla said was true, I'd better not do any falling off; but if Easter was anything to go by, that was unlikely. Still, for now, I had to get on with tacking up Bilbo or I'd be in trouble. Bilbo's tack was at the other end of the room from Tim's and at the other end of the scale, too. It was clean enough, but the saddle was stiff and almost black, not a bit like Tim's soft, pliable brown one. There was a sheepskin rug hanging on the hook. I didn't know what it was for so I left it there. Even the bridle was yucky – the reins were made of horrible braided material instead of leather, and felt sticky.

I balanced the saddle over my right arm and draped the bridle over it, the way you do, and carted it all over to Bilbo. I hadn't bothered to really say hello to him because I'd been too busy catching him and then feeling annoyed with him, and now he gave me a sidelong glare that convinced me that he felt at least as unhappy about having me as I did about having him. I dumped the tack on the fence and put out a tentative hand to pat his flank. He started as if I'd hit him.

"Great," I muttered, and started to put on his tack.

As I buckled his saddle, I ran my fingers along the smooth strap to check that Bilbo's tummy wasn't being pinched. Satisfied that I'd chosen the right hole for the buckle, I then let him mouth the metal bar and the bit, and slipped the bridle over his head. I felt much calmer and more content. Bilbo might be a second-best after

Tim, but, hey, he was a pony, and we were just about to set out on a fantastic three-day ride. The sun was shining, and the wonderful horsy smells and the sounds – hoofs clattering, bits jingling, ponies snorting – were the ones I'd dreamed of all summer.

"Tack inspection," called Mr. Butler.

He came along the line, checking girths and looking for problems. A couple of people had made mistakes, and I hoped so much that I'd be OK. I was last. I held my breath as he checked.

"Fine," he said, and I breathed again. Then he looked again and added, as if he thought I was a total idiot, "Oh Jess, you've forgotten his numnah. It's the special rug he wears under the saddle to protect his back. Go and get it and we'll all wait for you."

The way he put it meant that I felt everyone's eyes on me as I collected the bit of sheepskin. Then I had to unsaddle Bilbo, put the blanket in place on his bony back, put the saddle back on, and do the girth up again – on a different hole now.

"That's better." Mr. Butler didn't actually sound annoyed with me; it was just that I felt so silly. I'd never really registered that some ponies had these blankets between their backs and the saddles. Camilla and Georgie were watching in their irritatingly superior way, and I was sure Emily was whispering something rude about me to Rosie.

Still, one of the things I'd learned at Easter, apart from how to ride a little, was not to be too sensitive to criticism. I'd spent so much time imagining everyone laughing at me, and in the end I'd realized that most of the time people were either sympathetic or just not that interested. So I was determined not to get upset, and carefully ignored the twins and Rosie and Emily for the next few minutes.

Caroline and Mr. Butler had been loading all the heavier gear onto Campbell, who looked very sweet. His dark eyes were just visible under his long, long mane and his back looked colorful with all the camping gear.

We were shown how to attach our saddlebags, one on each side in front of the leg flaps, and our rolled-up sleeping bags went on top of the saddles in front of us. We each also had a big water bottle. Mrs. Butler came out with a tray of cold drinks and doughnuts, and then it was time to start.

"Everybody mount!" yelled Caroline.

It was like something from a film. Almost in unison, we each stood by the left sides of our ponies, facing away from their heads. We gathered the reins in our left hands and put our left feet into the stirrups. We each held the reins in one of our hands and the saddle pommels in the other, and lifted ourselves into the saddles, our right legs swinging up and over and then neatly down and into the opposite stirrups. The ponies shuffled and fidgeted, excited that the trip was about to begin.

Most of us leaned down to change the length of the stirrup leathers. Mine were uneven so it took a while to get them right, and then I couldn't decide if they were too long or not. They felt OK, so I thought I'd leave them. I settled into the saddle and immediately realized that Bilbo felt quite different from Tim. The saddle protected me from Bilbo's bony back, but his sides were so much narrower than Tim's. It made me feel totally different. Then I noticed that his mane was short and started much further up his neck, so there was no comforting mass of soft hair to cover my fingers or to hold onto if I felt insecure. Anyway, the bulky sleeping bag made a barrier between my hands and his neck. And, of course, he was black instead of gray, and once I was sitting on him, that seemed far more obvious.

Tim walked past. Georgie was sitting very upright and looking professional. She was holding his reins tightly and Tim's head was high. I remembered how Tim had spent most of my first day putting his head down to snatch mouthfuls of grass, and tightened Bilbo's reins, too.

"Not too tight, Jess," said Caroline, next to me. "He doesn't like to have his mouth hurt. Just feel the pressure gently."

So how come she hadn't told Georgie off? Still, I let the reins thread through my fingers a little just as Bilbo shook his head. I wobbled in the saddle but my feet were firmly in the stirrups. I was all right.

"Everybody ready?" called Caroline, swinging herself onto Micky and winding Campbell's halter rope around her left hand. "Walk on!"

Before I had time to feel really ready, the ponies had responded by following out onto the lane. Bilbo jostled himself into a spot

36

behind Bramble. Phil turned around, his hand on the back of the saddle to balance himself, and grinned happily.

"OK, Jess?"

"Fantastic," I said, though I was actually feeling kind of uncertain. Was I controlling Bilbo or was he controlling me?

Before I had time to find out, the line of ponies and riders was on the wide path alongside the quiet lane that led away from the farmhouse toward the hills. I twisted around to see who was behind me, and had a quick glimpse of Megan on Star, when Caroline called out again.

"Trot on!"

Bilbo didn't wait for me to give him any signal. He launched straight into a fast, bumpy trot – and I flew straight into the air, and hit the ground shoulder first amid a flurry of hoofs. Then everything went black.

Chapter Four

When I opened my eyes, a sea of faces surrounded me. It was hard to focus and my brain felt fuzzy. Then, as if I was swimming up through deep water, I remembered what had happened and was immediately terrified that I'd be off the trek.

"Gently does it." I recognized Mrs. Butler's motherly voice. Someone brought a wet cloth and she put it against my head. "Does that hurt?"

"No," I lied. I knew I didn't want to miss any riding. "I'm fine."

"Are you sure? You came down with an awful thump."

"I'm sure." I sat up, and touched my shoulder. It was sore but there was no blood or anything.

"What about your arm? Can you move it?"

"Yes. Everything's fine. Can I get back on Bilbo now?"

Mrs. Butler put a restraining hand on me. "Sorry, but we'll have to have you checked out. You might have gotten a concussion."

"I didn't! I promise I didn't! I'm all right."

"The doctor's on his way." Caroline knelt down next to me. "How do you feel?"

"I'm fine!" I protested again. "Please…"

It didn't make any difference. The whole group had to go back to the yard, untack the ponies, and hang around, while I was told to wait indoors with my feet up on the sofa until the doctor arrived. They must not have told him it was urgent, because he took forever to get there. We'd had sandwiches and the others had played a game of football in the paddock before his car eventually rolled into the yard.

He checked me over and looked into my eyes with a little flashlight.

"You're sure you never lost consciousness?" he asked.

"Totally," I lied. There was no way I was going to admit to that few seconds of blackness if it might mean delaying the trek or even being forbidden to go on it.

He examined my shoulder, which had turned a pale shade of pinky-purple, and said I'd only bruised it.

"It'll hurt for a while," he warned. "It might be stiff tomorrow and the next day."

"Doesn't matter," I said, a bit tensely because actually it was hurting a lot, especially where he'd touched it.

The doctor turned to Mr. and Mrs. Butler. "She'll be all right," he said. "These riders of yours are tough; they don't give up easily, do they?"

He patted my unhurt shoulder cheerfully and left.

"Can I get up now?" I asked.

"If you're quite sure you're feeling OK," said Mrs. Butler, anxiously.

Determined not to show any pain, I stood up and stretched. It did hurt, and my head ached a bit, but I smiled and said I was fine. Then I saw the other riders just outside the window. They'd obviously been told not to come in and were waiting to hear what would happen next.

I waved and grinned. They all looked relieved. Then we went outside and started getting the ponies ready again. Rosie gave me a comforting hug and most of the others smiled sympathetically, though Emily and Georgie looked annoyed. I heard Emily say something that sounded like, "incompetent beginners."

"It's half past two, and we've lost quite a lot of time," announced Mr. Butler. "So we'll take a shorter route than we intended and we won't get to the camping place till around seven. Everyone OK with that?"

There was a chorus of assent. There wasn't likely not to be, I thought, as I got ready, with a sinking feeling in my stomach, to mount Bilbo again. They've all been held up for so long they're not going to want any more delays, especially not from incompetent beginners like me.

To add to my shame, Caroline clipped a leading rein to Bilbo's noseband before jumping onto Micky.

"I don't need that," I started, but she shushed me.

"It won't be for long. Just until we're away from the road and you feel in control."

"But –"

"No buts. Either you have the leading rein or you don't come." It was Mr. Butler, towering over us on Captain. "I'll take Campbell for now, Caroline."

I was hot with embarrassment and anger that I should be treated like a complete novice. Hadn't I spent a full week – well, five days – riding Tim, trotting, cantering, and even just starting jumping? Why did they suddenly want to treat me like a fool?

I held Bilbo's reins loosely when we finally set off. What was the point of trying to guide him when Caroline was doing all the work? When we got to where I'd fallen off, I stiffened in the saddle and my shoulder felt suddenly sorer, but once we were past the spot I felt better. I was at the end of the procession of ponies, so no one was looking at me, and it was actually nice to be able to take the time to feel comfortable on horseback again, without worrying about taking charge of Bilbo. He still felt very thin between my legs and I found it disconcerting not to be able to grab a chunk of mane when he stumbled suddenly. The braided reins began to feel less strange. I even leaned forward and patted his smooth neck. There were paler hairs among the black ones, so the overall effect was a dark brown. He had white socks on all four legs. I thought about grooming him this evening and how satisfying it would be to brush out the loose hairs and rub the others till they shone. So long as he didn't bite me, that is.

We trekked down the lane for ages. Caroline told me it was because we were taking a shortcut. Although it was kind of boring, and it meant I had to stay on the leading rein, it did give me a long time to get used to riding again. And because we stayed in the same long line all the time, I didn't have to worry about the others feeling sorry for me or despising me. I didn't know which was worse.

Micky and Bilbo trotted side by side quite happily.

"Aren't you worried Bilbo will bite Micky?" I asked.

"He's just a little naughty. You don't need to worry much about it. Just be sure to keep him away from the other ponies when they're wandering around in the yard. It's when he's bored that he nips."

"Oh. Right."

I'd somehow gotten it into my head that Bilbo was almost a monster, but of course they'd never use him at the farm if he were really bad-tempered. I thought back to Easter. Bilbo hadn't really done anything too bad. Maybe he'd been bored and wanted some excitement. It can't be much fun sometimes, carting assorted children around, some of them sawing at your mouth or kicking you too hard. My lovely Tim was sweet natured and patient, but I supposed not every pony could be like that. I even wondered if a little mischief and friskiness might not be kind of fun.

So I was much happier by the time we finally left the lane and started down a long track. Tall trees on either side shaded us from the hot sun. Caroline drew Micky to a quiet stop and Bilbo automatically stood still next to him.

"How do you feel, Jess? Are you OK on your own? What about your arm?"

I flexed my shoulder. To be honest, it was really sore, but I said it hardly hurt. "I think I'll be all right with Bilbo now," I added. "I've remembered what riding feels like."

"Well, don't rush to do everything right off the bat," she advised, leaning sideways to unclip the leading rein, and then coiling it loosely and attaching it to her saddle. "When we canter, remember to stay with me and I'll take care of you."

"Thanks," I said. Of course, it was nice of her to be so kind, but I wished she'd just leave me alone. Everyone else was chatting and making friends, and I'd been isolated the whole time. Emily and Rosie were talking together non-stop, and I couldn't help feeling jealous.

Now that I was free, I gathered the reins in my fingers and squeezed with my heels. Bilbo walked obediently after the other ponies. I was a long way behind, so I dared myself to trot and gave him a gentle kick. He didn't bother to respond, so I kicked more sharply. Bilbo tossed his head but went into a trot. I lurched forward for a second, pushed myself back with a hand on his withers – his shoulder – and settled into the saddle.

Last time I'd learned how to rise to the trot. The technical word is posting. You really do need to do it, or else you can get totally sore – ponies are pretty bouncy when they trot. I'd gotten the hang of Tim's trot, and the special way you have to rise just when you'd expect to fall so that the magic smooth rhythm can establish itself. While Caroline had led me, I'd managed to rise OK. On my own, it was more difficult, because I was trying to hold Bilbo in and guide him at the same time. We jogged in a disorganized and haphazard way until we reached the others. Bilbo decided he didn't want to be at the back anymore, and took me past Emily and Rosie at a fast trot. I nearly yelled out for someone to catch me and slow me down, but I didn't want to look incompetent. So I pulled the reins a little more, and tried to sit down well into the saddle. Maybe because of me or maybe because he just wanted to, Bilbo slowed down and I found myself walking sedately next to Megan on Star.

"Hi," I said, breathlessly. I wanted to give the impression that I'd chosen to end up next to her.

"Are you OK now?" she asked, sounding worried.

I sighed. "It was just a fall," I said. "Happens to everyone."

"A dramatic one, though. There was an awful crack as you landed."

"Was there? Must have been a twig or something. It hardly hurt at all."

"If you say so." Megan didn't look very convinced, but she seemed to be tactful enough to drop it. We started telling each other about ourselves. She was from a small town and lived with her mother and her two brothers. I was wondering whether her parents were divorced when she said sadly,

"Dad died last year."

"That's awful. What happened? Was he sick?"

"No, he was in a car accident. I miss him a lot. He was always laughing, you know? Mom's so serious."

"I'm so sorry. What about your brothers? How old are they?"

"Jamie's twelve and Ethan's ten. They're OK, but they spend a lot of time together, playing soccer and stuff. I like soccer, but not non-stop."

"My brother and sister are still too little for that," I said. I told her about Tim and Holly, and how they'd be having their first birthday soon. "I hated them at first," I added. "In fact, it was coming here that helped me realize how much I love them. They're really cute."

"They sound it. What about school? Who's your best friend?"

We talked and talked. We liked the same music, but she was much more athletic than I am, and I was more into shopping and clothes. She was just about to start tenth grade too, and was taking almost the same subjects as me.

She didn't mention her dad again, so I left the topic alone. I decided to come back to it if I could another time, in case she wanted to talk about it.

We were so engrossed that I didn't think about riding. In fact, when I suddenly remembered, I felt really smug. I was sitting correctly, with my heels down in the stirrups and the reins just taut enough but giving with each pace, as the pony's head went forward. I was perfectly balanced, too.

Maybe this is the answer, I thought. Riding by instinct instead of worrying non-stop. As if to prove me right, Bilbo stumbled, and I had to gather him together by tightening the reins, and by sitting especially well down in the saddle with my legs gripping the saddle flaps hard. Because I wasn't worrying about riding, I just did it and everything was all right.

Megan didn't even seem to notice, and we went on talking. We'd finally gotten to the end of the track and were following the contours of a hill. After a while, we turned downhill. Phil came up beside me.

"How're you doing?" he asked. "You didn't look too happy about getting Bilbo. It wasn't fair not letting you ride Tim, was it? I'd have been furious."

"It's OK now that I'm getting used to him," I said. I wasn't going to show any weaknesses to Phil. He was much too happy to complain, and I didn't need to give him any ammunition.

We didn't say anymore. The hill was steep and I had to concentrate. I wanted to lean back but remembered being told not to. I sat up very straight and sort of felt my weight through the stirrups. I had to let out the reins to give Bilbo a chance to see where he was going, but when he skidded slightly I felt really insecure. I grabbed the saddle pommel and a handful of the numnah underneath. Luckily, he didn't slide any more.

We got to the river at the bottom of the valley. It was so pretty, shallow and fast-running. Mr. Butler told us to dismount to give the ponies a breather and a chance to drink. I slid off and unbuckled Bilbo's bridle, taking care to hang on to the halter rope so I could hold onto him while he drank. I also took care to move a little to one side, so that he wouldn't be tempted to bite me. Caroline nodded approval at me. My legs felt wobbly now that I was back on the ground, and my shoulder hurt, but the headache had gone and the water was cool outside my boots. Further up, Tom and Camilla were scrambling around in the middle of the stream, dragging their ponies behind them as they jumped from rock to rock. Everyone was laughing and happy.

"Just like last time."

It was Rosie, pulling Twinkle along.

"Kate and Ed didn't last together for long, though, did they?" I said.

On my first ride at Easter, we'd been having lunch by a stream just like this one when Kate had started a play fight with a boy called Ed. They'd gotten soaked, so they'd been sent back to the farm. Not that they minded. They liked each other a lot, and Kate had spent most of the rest of the week annoying Rosie by ignoring her in favor of Ed. That incident had been the start of all my troubles with Mike, too, as, while Mr. Butler was away, he dared a boy called Chris to ride Captain. I had helped Chris, and became Public Enemy Number One.

"Let's hope this week we can have just as much fun without all the stress," said Rosie.

"Umm." I agreed, but a bit of me thought, you haven't helped so far by cozying up to Emily. No sooner had I thought of her than she appeared. Mr. Man was a truly adorable pony, all shaggy long

45

mane and clumpy feet. He seemed very easygoing, too. Emily was dragging him along behind her without a thought for whether he wanted to follow. I put a hand on Bilbo's smooth neck and patted him, and he turned his head towards me and gave me a look that seemed, if not exactly friendly, at least not hostile.

"We'll do fine," I murmured to him, and his ears pricked as if he was listening and understanding.

Emily had started talking to Rosie in a very possessive way about their previous stay at the farm, leaving me out of the conversation completely, so Bilbo and I moved away. We stood six inches deep in the stream. Bilbo kept putting his head down and then lifting it to have a look around. His muzzle dripped and he snorted once or twice to get rid of the water in his nose. I liked the way he looked around. He seemed alert and intelligent.

I watched the others further downstream. Tom and Camilla were deep in conversation. Phil was chatting to Megan. Georgie was on her own, stroking Tim. I felt a stab of longing. OK, I was getting to like Bilbo more, but I'd still have preferred to ride Tim. I even felt a little guilty that I was making friends with Bilbo, as if I was betraying Tim. It struck me that Georgie didn't look too happy, either, but I wasn't going to make any special efforts for her. I'd decided very quickly that she and Camilla were just not my type of people. They wouldn't want to be friends with someone like me, anyway.

Caroline told everyone to put the bridles back on and remount.

"We'll be cantering, so you need to check your girths first and maybe adjust your leathers," she called.

My tummy lurched. Cantering was something I'd done a few times, and it had felt great, but it also felt very scary, and I wasn't at all sure I was ready for it.

I'd loosened the saddle girth when we stopped anyway, so now I pulled the heavy buckle till it felt right. Then I checked by running my fingers between it and Bilbo's tummy. There's supposed to be room for four fingers. It was a little too tight, so I loosened it again. Mr. Butler came and checked and said I'd gotten it right.

"Are you OK to canter?" he said. "You don't have to, especially after your fall this morning."

46

I saw Emily nearby. She was obviously listening. No way was I going to show any weakness in front of her.

"No, I want to," I answered. I was mounting as I spoke and feeling for the right-hand stirrup. "These stirrups feel uneven. Did I get them right?"

"Let's have a look." Mr. Butler stood in front of Bilbo, looking at both sides. "Well, they're even, but they're too long, I'd say. Wasn't it uncomfy when you were trotting?"

"A bit, but I thought that was just me. I haven't done any real riding since Easter."

"You're right, it feels strange when you start again. Especially on a different pony. But you'll be much better with shorter leathers. Let's see what I can do."

Obediently, I stuck each leg forward in turn so that he could lift the saddle flap and pull up the straps.

"They're on the fourth hole from the top now, but the third should be OK when we're not cantering. See how they feel."

I inserted my feet into the stirrups. They seemed miles higher, as if my knees were up parallel with my nose. Like a jockey, I thought, but I didn't want to make any stupid remarks. Mr. Butler went to check the others.

Phil came up on Bramble.

"Do you think my stirrups are too short?" I asked, anxiously.

He considered carefully, moving Bramble so he could look from in front, just like Mr. Butler.

"Maybe a bit," he said. "Why don't you change them?"

"Mr. Butler put them like this."

Phil shrugged. "He probably knows what he's doing. Jess, I've been trying to talk to you alone all day. You never called."

Luckily, Mr. Butler signalled for us to start at that moment so I didn't have to think up any explanation. The truth was, I hadn't known whether to call Phil or not. He'd been kind and a good friend, but he'd also been such a complainer. I wasn't sure I wanted to start some sort of romance, but I was fairly certain he did.

The ponies' hoofs made a lovely thudding sound as we trotted in a cheerful group along the grassy valley. The stream splashed next to us and gleamed as the sun caught it. Mr. Butler led us. Caroline

47

stayed at the back, with Georgie next to her, talking earnestly about something. The rest of us rode together, the ponies' heads jogging from side to side as they looked at their friends, their actions smooth and rhythmic except for the occasional small stumble. We riders were rising and falling steadily and keeping eyes out on the ground ahead for bumps.

Bilbo pulled on the reins as if he wanted to go faster. I pulled back and sat down into the saddle to slow him. He shook his head impatiently, and the reins shot through my fingers. At the same moment, he seemed to take my sitting as an indication that he should start to canter. I felt a stretching of the muscles under my legs as he thrust his legs forward. To my horror, he launched into a fast, smooth, terrifying canter.

Chapter Five

The other ponies seemed to think that Bilbo had a good idea. Hanging on with my legs, my hands, and my desperate hope not to fall off again, I soon realized that Star, Twinkle, Magpie, Mr. Man, Bramble and Rolo were racing Bilbo through the valley. Their riders all seemed thrilled, judging from the excited shouts. I risked a quick glance sideways and saw Tom leaning forward, his face pressed against Rolo's gray neck. Beyond him, Camilla was bouncing her legs energetically against Magpie's sides, urging him on. Bilbo swerved suddenly and I concentrated on staying on. Every muscle in my body was tense and straining. I could feel a rush of air against my face, and my mouth was becoming drier every second. Bilbo stumbled again, and my left foot slipped from the stirrup. Instinctively, panic-stricken, I thrust it back and almost instantly felt the solid metal underneath again. I looked down to check and wished at once that I hadn't. The ground was whizzing by at a terrific rate, and Bilbo's white socks flashed as he rushed along. I shut my eyes and hoped.

Suddenly, everything seemed to go into slow motion. I opened my eyes. The ground had slowed down. Bilbo was bumping along, and then the motion subsided into the quiet side-to-side sway of a walk. I dared to look up and around. We were approaching a fence that barred the way forward. All the ponies gathered together there, panting and sweating. Their riders looked exhilarated.

"That was totally awesome!"

"Amazing."

"Best gallop I've ever had."

Gallop? I saw Rosie not far away and walked Bilbo gently over to her. I knew I was trembling and hoped nothing showed.

"Was that a gallop?" I asked quietly.

"I think so." She sounded awed. "I've never ever gone that fast on a pony. Wasn't it something?"

"Something else." I wasn't going to admit to how terrified I'd been if everyone else was so happy.

Captain, Micky, Campbell and Tim were trotting sedately towards us.

"That wasn't precisely what I had in mind for the first canter of the vacation," said Mr. Butler, but he was smiling. "Everyone OK?"

We all said we were, including me. Well, I was, wasn't I? I'd cantered – no, I'd galloped – and I hadn't fallen off or even completely lost a stirrup.

"Another time, wait till you get the signal to start, though, Jess," he added.

I turned red. I knew, and I knew he knew, that the whole thing had been unintentional, and that Bilbo had taken charge of me. But so what? I'd managed.

"Great gallop," said Camilla, circling Magpie past me.

"Oh. Yeah, it was," I managed to say. Wow – maybe she'd be friendly now that I'd shown I could ride. She went over to her sister and said something, and they both giggled. My confidence took a nosedive. Not so friendly after all. But I pushed the thought from my mind and concentrated on sorting out Bilbo. I lengthened the stirrups by a notch and wriggled in the saddle till I felt right. I gathered the reins together and gave his neck a pat.

A pat that wasn't quite friendship and trust yet, but it was on its way there.

Caroline opened the field gate and we filed through. I was careful to steer Bilbo away from the gatepost. Once a pony's halfway through, you can find your leg squashed between its body and the hard post if you're not alert, and while I was feeling more relaxed with Bilbo, I wasn't sure he wouldn't try something,

51

especially since he was excited and fidgety after the gallop. The gate led to a narrow lane – so underused that grass grew down the center – that wound slowly uphill. The ponies clattered along at a gentle walk. There was general conversation – jokes and silly remarks and a feeling of contented friendship – that passed up and down the line so everyone could hear and take part. After a while, Mr. Butler stopped by a wide opening in the hedge.

"Down there's the camping area," he announced.

There was a wide field of grass, low bushes and the occasional tree. A stream – maybe the same one as before – made a wide circle almost enclosing it. All around, the hills were steep and bushy. The colors – greens and pinks and yellows and the pale blue sky – were wonderful.

Rosie said, in a doom-laden voice, "If we camp in the middle, and it rains, we'll get flooded."

Caroline laughed. "Come off it, Rosie, it's been boiling hot all week. It's not going to rain tonight. Look at the sky."

"Red sky at night, sailor's delight," put in Megan.

"Exactly. Though it's not really late enough for that yet. We'll have a couple of hours of daylight before it's too dark to see what we're doing."

"Help!" yelped Emily. "How on earth are we meant to get the tents set up in time?"

"Or the food cooked," added Tom. "I'm starving."

"Let's not waste any more time, then," suggested Mr. Butler. "The quickest way's down the hillside, but it's steep for the ponies, so you can choose either to make your way downhill really slowly and carefully or to keep going on this lane. Off we go."

The party split. Tom, Georgie, Camilla, Megan and Phil started down the hill, and Caroline closed the gap behind them with some wire. I decided to stick with the adults. I wasn't sure I could trust Bilbo to go gently – he might decide to gallop and throw me again. Rosie came with me, muttering something about flash floods.

"What are you talking about?" I asked.

"You must have heard about flash floods. They come from nowhere and the water level goes way up. Then everyone gets swept away."

"But you heard what Mr. Butler said. We're safe here."

Rosie didn't look convinced.

We went through another gate. The whole camping area was enclosed by a post and rail fence, with the stream meandering through the center. The others were still picking their way down through the bushes. Mr. Butler told us to dismount and untack. We used the halter ropes to tie the ponies to the fence. Bilbo's back was dark and sweaty under the rug, and his bit was covered in frothy saliva. I felt sorry for him, carrying me all day up and down hills. I gave him a hug.

"Ouch!"

"What's the matter?"

"He bit me!"

Caroline came over and looked at my bare arm. There was a red mark but the skin wasn't broken.

"Don't worry, you'll live," she said. "You should have been more careful. You know what he's like."

"I thought we'd made friends," I said. I could feel hot tears at the back of my eyes, and I shook my head fiercely to push them back.

"I'm sure you have. Just remember he's a pony that nips when he's bored or tired. He probably wanted to remind you that he's hungry."

True, Bilbo had used this opportunity to get his head down and start munching the short sweet grass. I dumped the sleeping bag and saddlebags on the ground and balanced his saddle onto the fence. I looked at the slimy saliva on the bit. I was going to have to clean that myself and there was no nice well-equipped stable yard here; just a stream and a load of grass. Suddenly, I felt incredibly tired.

"That was wicked," said Tom, cantering Rolo up to us and stopping with a flurry of hoofs. "We sort of sideslipped all the way down, like skiing. Can we have another try?"

"Not tonight. The ponies have had enough. But there'll be plenty of hills to come," promised Mr. Butler. He looked up at the slope. "Are you OK?" he yelled.

Georgie was coming down at a snail's pace. Tim was going almost straight downhill, and you could see his hoofs slipping on every other step. Georgie looked scared. For someone who rode a lot, I thought she was surprisingly nervous. She was the only one who hadn't galloped, too.

"I'll get her," said Camilla, and before anyone could say anything, she'd jumped back onto Magpie and was trotting him uphill at a steep angle. We watched as she joined her twin, grabbed Tim's halter and led them down in a series of zigzags. When they reached us, Georgie was red in the face and complaining about Tim. I felt furious with her. No one had made her have Tim, and here she was whining about him.

"Don't blame your pony," I heard myself saying. "It's almost always the rider who's at fault."

"Quite right, Jess, though you didn't seem so sure about that a minute ago when Bilbo bit you," said Mr. Butler.

There was a ripple of laughter and it was my turn to redden. Luckily, there wasn't time to get flustered or have arguments. Caroline was organizing everyone.

"Once you've untacked, give the ponies a quick rubdown and then let them loose. Wash off the bits and leave them on the fence to dry next to the saddles. Then come over here and we'll start pitching camp."

"Too much like hard work," grumbled Phil, tying Bramble to the fence near me.

As usual, the effect of Phil's complaining was to make me more cheerful.

"It's got to be done," I said, brushing Bilbo's sides energetically. Dust flew from him. "Where on earth does all this come from?"

"It's always the same with black ponies," said Megan, who was untacking Star on my other side. "Look."

Star was black too, apart from the four-pointed marking that sat prettily between her eyes. Megan was right; dust rose from Star, too.

We all three carried the bridles down to the stream to wash them. Caroline, who seemed to be everywhere this evening, directed us downstream, so that the froth and dirt wouldn't pollute our campsite's water.

"We're not drinking it, though, are we?" I said. It was a clean enough stream, but bits of vegetation and tiny fish were everywhere.

54

"No, they wouldn't make us, would they?" Phil gasped, horror-struck.

Megan winked at me and said, "Well, you never know. We are camping in the wild, after all."

"But the ponies are drinking from it!"

"Ask Caroline," Megan advised.

We giggled as Phil sprinted over to ask Caroline. She shook her head, of course. I have to admit, I was relieved, too. Drinking that water would be gross.

A few minutes later, the long line of ponies, their bare backs freshly brushed, had been released and were jostling companionably down to the water. Most of them stood fetlock-deep, drinking deeply and then lifting dripping muzzles to gaze around at the unfamiliar surroundings. A few had already left the water and, heads down, were filling their bellies with sweet grass.

Mr. Butler had unpacked the bundles that Campbell had carried all day. There were six orange rolled-up tents, a bundle of cooking gear, an insulated bag and a huge water bottle.

"Can we have something to drink? I'm dying of thirst," said Emily.

"Fill your water bottles from the big one, but don't waste any or we'll run out. We can't get any more tap water till tomorrow."

Remembering the alternative was the stream water, we took turns to fill our individual bottles really carefully.

"That'll make things a lot lighter for poor old Campbell," commented Rosie.

"He's better off than Twinkle, even with all that water," said Camilla sweetly yet snottily.

"That's enough of that," said Caroline, crossly. Camilla looked embarrassed. Her dig at Rosie for being a little hefty had backfired, since Caroline was much larger.

Mr. Butler showed us where to pitch our tents, inside the almost-circle made by the stream. I grabbed a tent and looked around for Rosie to help me, but she was talking to Phil. Meanwhile, Megan dumped a tent at Emily's feet and said something to her. Emily turned red and Megan looked annoyed. Rosie wandered back over and we started putting up the tent. It wasn't too hard – the frame

55

was inside, and all you had to do was attach a few pieces together. Rosie went around the outside, hammering tent stakes into the ground to keep it stable while I crawled inside with the sleeping bags. It was a warm, cozy, slightly claustrophobic space. The light filtered through as unnatural orange, and the smell was clean and plasticky. There wasn't much room, just enough for the two sleeping bags spread out on the floor and a space between for our saddlebags and water. I thought about how much fun it was going to be in the dark, whispering to each other. I carefully took out my flashlight and put it where my head would lie, for later.

A voice rose outside.

"Don't tell me what to do!" it screamed.

I poked my head out through the tent opening. Rosie was halfway between our tent and the next one, where Megan was holding up tent material and Emily was scrambling to attach poles, her face red and angry. Megan didn't look exactly happy, either.

"Well, do it right, then," she said. She sounded really irritated.

"I am!" shouted Emily. "You're holding the wrong piece."

"No, I'm not!"

"You are!"

"Girls, girls!" Mr. Butler looked really fed up. "What on earth's the matter?"

"It's Megan," complained Emily, loudly. "She doesn't know what she's doing."

"As if!" replied Megan hotly. "All you've done is mess around and whine."

"Well, you're going to have to sort it out," said Mr. Butler. "You two are partners; the other girls came in pairs. So you'll have to make up and work together."

There was a sulky silence. Megan and Emily started again, each pointedly not looking at each other, while Mr. Butler watched them from a distance.

I tied the tent entrance flap open so I could sit cross-legged on the tarp. Nibbling a long stalk of grass, I looked around. The sun was going down and the light across the campsite was pink and gold and quite beautiful. All around me I could hear the sound of tent stakes being hammered into place, the chatter of each pair putting up their tent, the clatter of frying pans as Caroline set up the camp kitchen, and the occasional whinny or snort from the ponies grazing nearby.

Rosie plonked herself down in front of me.

"Em's really upset," she said. "You don't mind if we swap and I share with her, do you?"

What could I say? Of course I minded. Rosie and I had come together as friends. On top of that, I couldn't help thinking that if Emily hadn't been encouraged to share our room last night, she might've been getting along better with Megan now. On the other hand, I felt sorry for Megan, and I liked her too. And saying "no' to Rosie might be unwise; I knew from experience that when Rosie was irritated she got to be difficult.

So I said, "OK," and Rosie squealed with joy as if sharing a tent with me was the worst thing ever. She pulled out her stuff and rushed off to her new best friend.

I sat there and thought about how things can change.

"Hi. I hope this is OK with you? I feel so bad about it..."

Megan was standing awkwardly, clutching all her possessions.

"Course it's OK. We'll have a great time," I said quickly, smiling at her reassuringly.

"You really and truly don't mind?"

"Not a bit. Rosie and I aren't that friendly anyway."

I squeezed to one side so that Megan could crawl past me into the tent. She spread out her sleeping bag, and I saw a furry panda peeping out from it.

"Hey, I've got my bear too," I said, suddenly not at all ashamed to have a teddy bear at my age, as long as someone else did too. We solemnly "introduced" them to each other, and then, giggling, zipped the tent shut and went to join the others.

Mr. Butler staggered toward the kitchen area, carrying a huge stack of twigs and small branches.

"Don't just stand there!" he said. "Go and get some fuel, if you want supper cooked and a good fire for later. You go too, twins."

"I can't imagine being cold enough for a fire," said Megan, as we wandered slowly toward the gate, beyond which were trees and lots of dry wood lying around.

"Um, it's still boiling."

Phil and Tom, who were leaping about energetically, joined us, fooling around and making us laugh. In the woods, where it was getting quite dark, they kept hiding behind tree trunks and jumping out at us. Then Tom decided that gathering wood at ground level was boring, so he climbed a tree and started throwing leaves and tiny twigs at us. Camilla and Georgie climbed up after Tom, and ended up balancing precariously on a long, low branch.

"I can't get down!" shrieked Camilla in mock horror.

"Slide!" advised Tom behind her.

They both sat astride the branch, and wriggled their way down till they were only head height above ground. Then Tom leaped down and Phil held out his arms and suggested Camilla jump into them. She did, and her weight pushed them both flat on the ground. They picked themselves up, laughing, brushing loads of dead leaves from their clothes and hair. I thought how much Phil had improved since Easter. He was hardly grumbling at all now.

Georgie was still halfway along the branch, looking a little scared. We all encouraged her to jump, and Phil volunteered to catch her.

"No way!" she said. "You just dropped Camilla."

"Sorry!" said Phil, shrugging and walking away.

"Edge along a bit, and you can put your foot onto my shoulder," I suggested, standing in the right place.

She shuffled along and slid sideways onto me. But I'd forgotten about the injury I'd had earlier – it had stopped hurting during the day. But Georgie's boot landed on the bruised area. I yelped and instinctively pulled away. Tears sprung to my eyes but I blinked hard and rubbed my shoulder quickly. I didn't want to make a big deal about it.

Meanwhile, Georgie was being really dramatic. She'd landed awkwardly, but the ground was soft, covered in old leaves and stuff, so she couldn't really have done much harm to herself. In fact, once Camilla and Tom had hauled her up and let her lean on them, she stood quite normally, but when she took a step she screamed that her knee hurt. They half carried her back to the camp while Phil, Megan and I followed.

The others ran towards us to see what was wrong. Mr. Butler made Georgie sit down. He examined her knee carefully.

"I don't think you've done any real damage," he said. "We'll put a bandage on it and see how you are in the morning, OK?"

Georgie nodded and for the rest of the evening she stayed in one place while people carried things for her.

Caroline had scooped out some grass, and on the bare ground beneath she'd built a fantastic fire. Rosie and Emily had helped her set up a tripod of thick branches above it and suspended a kettle of water, which was already starting to steam. Carefully, she took it off the heat and gave us all thick metal skewers with wooden handles.

"Put as many hot dogs as you want onto the skewers and hold them near the embers," she instructed.

The fire was really hot, and we had to be careful not to scorch either the hot dogs or ourselves. Once the hot dogs were done, all smoky and smelling amazing, we pushed them into enormous buns and stuffed ourselves till we were almost bursting. After-wards there were slices of ginger cake and crunchy apples.

Then Mr. Butler put the kettle on for a few more minutes and used the boiling water to make a jug of hot chocolate. We lounged around the campfire in the gathering dark, our stomachs full, warm and contented, talking vaguely of this and that, but mostly of horses. Stars gradually appeared in the sky. The ponies were now just dark shapes in the distance, indistinguishable from each other.

"Time for bed," Mr. Butler said at last. "You'll probably wake up early, so get some sleep now."

The girls gathered together at one end of the field – Caroline and Camilla helped Georgie – and the boys disappeared to the other side, so that we could all go to the bathroom. Then we went down to the stream to wash. It was magic – black water chattering over the rocks, gleaming by flashlight. We wandered back to the tents and crawled into our sleeping bags, calling good night to the other tents, snuggling up and watching the triangle of night sky at the open end of the tent.

"Let's leave it open," Megan said, and I agreed.

Caroline's form obscured the sky as she leaned over to check that we were OK. Then everything went quiet, apart from the soft, disjointed murmur of voices from other tents, the gentle crackling of the dying camp fire, the muffled clomp of a pony moving, and an eerie, beautiful owl hoot that filled the night for a moment and then was no more.

Chapter Six

Whenever I'd been camping before, I'd had some sort of mattress to lie on. I'd had no idea how knobby and hard the ground becomes when you lie on it for a few hours. But I was so tired that all I'd do was wake, turn over, wriggle into a better position, and fall asleep again.

When I opened my eyes, the tent was glowing bright orange. For a moment, I actually thought it was on fire, and leaned across to shake Megan awake. Then I realized it was just the early morning sun. Megan grunted but didn't wake up. I sat up cautiously and looked at my watch. 6:30 a.m.

Normally, I'd go straight back to sleep, but that seemed to be a waste here. I crawled out of the bag and pulled on my pants – we'd slept in our underwear. I dug around in the saddlebag for my sweatshirt, as it was still cool, and crept outside.

The field was almost invisible. A mist had risen and covered the grass in a silky white blanket. I collected my boots from under the tiny vestibule and pushed them on, and then went out to explore. All the ponies were down by the stream, in a sleepy still group. Their legs emerged fantastically from the mist, and steam rose around them as the heat of the sun burned the mist away. I ran down towards them, grabbing a handful of long grass, and held it out, clicking my tongue in the special way you use to encourage horses or to let them know you're a friend. Tim turned his lovely gray head and saw me. Immediately, he pushed past the other ponies and came to me. His soft muzzle pushed gently against me, as if to say hi. Then he took the grass carefully from me. It stuck out absurdly like a pantomime moustache and then disappeared as he nibbled at it. I patted and hugged his sweet-smelling neck, flipping his mane away so I could kiss him. Then I felt the strong muscles move and he dropped his head to the grass and started to eat.

The other ponies had come over, curious and anxious for attention. Bilbo was among them, and a stab of guilt went through me. I bent over to pick some more grass to offer to him; the grass was very short, but he didn't have to turn his head away quite so disdainfully. OK, I thought, don't bother with me and I won't bother with you. Ignoring Bilbo, I sat down on a convenient rock among the ponies and just enjoyed being with them again – their smell, the sounds they made, everything about them.

Voices drifted over. The others were getting up. The mist had almost evaporated now, and the sun was really hot. Caroline was already lighting the fire and putting the kettle on to boil. I stood up and jogged uphill to the tents. There was a shout of laughter, and I realized that everyone had stopped what they were doing to look at me. Why? Had I done something stupid, like forget to get fully dressed?

A push in my back nearly had me on the ground. I staggered, recovered, and looked around. Close behind me, all the ponies were following me up to the tents.

"Look, it's the Pied Piper!" called Tom.

"They're ponies, not rats," protested Rosie.

"Course they are. Don't be so literal," he said dismissively. "Hey, Jess, you could do a circus act."

"Yeah, she looks like a clown," added Emily bitchily.

"Could be useful when it comes to catching them," said Phil, ignoring Emily. "Can you keep them all together like that?"

"I didn't do anything!" I said, laughing. "They just decided to follow me."

"Animal magic," said Tom, solemnly. "You could make a fortune."

As he spoke, there was a jostling movement behind me. As smoothly as if they had been trained, the ponies turned in a group, and cantered together to the far end of the field, where they halted.

Poised against the backdrop of the woods, they relaxed and began to eat the grass.

"Wow, how did you do that?" asked Megan.

"I really didn't do anything," I said. "I just gave Tim some grass."

Someone drew in breath quickly and I knew without looking it would be Georgie.

"And the other ponies too," I added as if I hadn't noticed. "They're so greedy. How's your knee this morning, Georgie?"

"It still hurts, but I'll be all right," she said.

"Just be careful," murmured Camilla, giving her a quick hug. The rest of us made sympathetic sounds.

"What about your shoulder, Jess?" asked Megan.

I smiled at her gratefully. Everyone else seemed to have forgotten about it.

"It's a bit sore, but not a problem," I said, flexing it. "I was lucky."

Georgie looked as if I'd annoyed her somehow. I couldn't think of why this could be, unless she didn't like someone else taking the limelight away from her.

The group broke up. Mr. Butler took charge, instructing us to take tents down, roll up sleeping bags, and help Caroline with the breakfast. After a few minutes' bustle, we were able to grab more mugs of hot chocolate and chunks of bread spread with cream cheese and slivers of ham. We stood chatting, as the grass was still damp. Rosie and Emily were close together, apparently the best of friends. They ignored me. I noticed that they'd both put on eye makeup, which seemed a little unnecessary under the circumstances, but then they started flirting with Tom and I understood why. Not that I blamed them. Tom was good-looking and fun, too, though I didn't actually like him myself. Before long, Camilla, Megan and Georgie had joined the other two girls, leaving me alone with Phil.

Phil was eating hungrily. At Easter, he'd been really picky about the food.

"Are you OK with this breakfast?" I asked.

"Yeah, it's fine. I like this sort of picnic food, don't you? It's big plates of meat and veggies all mixed up together that I hate."

64

"I see. You'll just have to go trekking every time you come here," I said.

"Umm, well, there's the downside. The ground was so hard last night, and it's disgusting having to go to the bathroom like, well, you know…"

I thought, why do you always spoil things? I didn't say anything, because I didn't want to make a big deal out of it, but I was disappointed. I really had thought that Phil was getting more sensible.

Soon Caroline and Mr. Butler were instructing us to do various chores – washing up in buckets of water from the stream, helping to pack the tents and cooking equipment on to Campbell's back, checking that nothing – especially trash – had been left behind. Then we each had to collect our ponies and groom them, before tacking up and putting our personal saddlebags and sleeping bags back on the saddles.

That all took forever – especially collecting the ponies, who'd evidently forgotten my Pied Piper effect. Luckily, Mr. Butler had some carrots, which we used to bribe the ponies. Embarrassingly, Tim trotted straight over to me and nuzzled my hand for his bit of carrot. Georgie, who'd been excused from most of the chores and was just hanging around, grabbed his head collar rope from me, looking annoyed. I thought she should have been pleased to not have to catch him herself. Bilbo was a little easier to catch than yesterday – unenthusiastic, but obedient. I tacked him up as efficiently as I could, but I had to admit that I didn't feel any warmth for him.

By the time we were ready to go, Rosie and Emily were clamoring for more to eat. Mr. Butler looked impatient, but Caroline produced some chocolate bars. Camilla and Megan said they didn't want any. Georgie, on the other hand, ate with enthusiasm. I went over to stroke Tim while she was otherwise occupied and thought how odd it was that she and Camilla were identical twins, and yet so easily told apart. Camilla had a fantastic figure, her long blonde hair framed her face beautifully, and she was always confident – though she could be snotty. Georgie had the same fair hair, but it was cut in a fringe that didn't flatter her rounder face. Her body was rounder, too, and sort of shapeless. I had the impression that she played second fiddle to her twin all the time, never as good at anything or as ready to take the lead in any situation. It made me think of my own twin siblings, Tim and Holly. They weren't identical, of course, being a boy and a girl, but it'd be fascinating to watch them develop different personalities as they grew up. And it could be difficult if one of them turned out to be more talented at something than the other.

"Concentrate on your own pony." Georgie untied Tim's halter rope and led him away from me, as if I was infectious or something.

"Sorry," I said, feeling guilty, but she ignored me. I ducked under Rolo's head and grabbed Bilbo's rope. I untied him quickly and mounted. He jiggled around unsettlingly, so I shortened the reins and sat down well in the saddle, while feeling for the stirrup with my right foot.

"Gently does it, Jess," said Mr. Butler, looking down at me from the great height of Captain. "He doesn't like to be held on too tight a rein. Lengthen them."

"Yes, but …"

"Don't argue."

"No, Mr. Butler."

Bilbo tossed his head dramatically as soon as I loosened the reins, and I felt scared and unsafe. I tightened them again and hoped that no one would notice. Then I kicked his sides carefully, just behind the girth, and he walked on, his neck nicely arched, his steps neat. I felt much more in control and very pleased with myself.

The others were ready now, too. We set off as usual, in a long line, a pony's length apart. I'd been careful to keep Bilbo away from the other ponies, and so far today he hadn't tried to bite. His black coat shone in the sunlight, and the warm pony smell combined with the comfortable jingle of harness and slight creak of the saddle to make me feel very happy, even if he wasn't my favorite pony. I was following Megan, who turned in the saddle every now and again to say something. Emily was just behind me, so I didn't bother to turn to her. She'd be far too busy talking to Rosie, the last in the line except for Mr. Butler.

Caroline, leading Campbell, led us back up the hill, keeping the pace slow to warm the ponies up. Then we struck off the lane onto a wide grassy track that wound steeply uphill. The view was amazing, and the air felt fresh and invigorating. It certainly felt that way to Bilbo, who strained at the bit, trying to go faster. I tightened the reins yet again. My hands were getting sore from holding him in, and my shoulder ached with the effort. He fidgeted and shook his head, and I started to worry that he'd launch into a gallop again the moment I let him. Megan said something and I hardly heard her, I was concentrating so much.

Then Caroline glanced back at the long line and called, "Everyone OK? Trot on!"

She could have waited for me to say no, I thought, as the line quickened into a fast trot. Bilbo didn't wait to be given the aids. Just like yesterday, I felt left behind as he started to trot fast. But at least this time I was more used to him. I stayed sitting well down, not trying to post till I was ready, and pulled the reins tighter again.

To my surprise, he stopped, so suddenly that I nearly went straight over his nose. The ponies ahead moved away fast, and the ones behind bypassed me. Rosie didn't even give me a sympathetic glance as she trotted neatly – and smugly – by.

"I told you not to hold him in too much, Jess," said Mr. Butler, looming over me. "You were trotting fine yesterday. What's gotten into you?"

"He keeps pulling," I said miserably.

"OK. Let's see what we can do. Sit straighter. You're leaning back. And make sure your lower legs are parallel to the stirrup leathers."

I looked down, and saw my feet were too far forward. I moved them back and straightened my shoulders. Things immediately felt more secure.

"Now, give the poor pony a bit of freedom. Are you worried he's going to run away with you?"

"A little."

"Well, you can always comfort yourself that you did fine yesterday. But there's a difference between letting him have his head and curbing him in. Poor old Bilbo – how would you like to have your neck held tightly like that?"

67

I released my hold on the braided reins and let them slide through my fingers. Bilbo tossed his head again, and I tensed at once.

"Don't panic," said Mr. Butler. "You're communicating your fear to the pony. He's just stretching, that's all. Now, you're looking good; shall we go?"

He flicked Bilbo gently with his riding crop, and Bilbo and Captain walked and then almost immediately trotted together.

"Go into a rising trot, or he might think you're asking for a canter," advised Mr. Butler.

I rose and fell, my teeth clenched with concentration, trying hard not to pull on the reins but to keep them steady. Bilbo responded with a nice even trot that felt controlled, although he was dropping his head, which I thought didn't look so good. That also meant that his neck was a long way from my hands and I didn't feel I'd be able to grab his mane if I started wobbling. The others were way ahead and I'd have been very bothered that Bilbo would canter or gallop to catch up if Captain hadn't been going along steadily next to me.

An ear-splitting scream pierced the air. Ahead of us, the tidy line dissolved into a messy group of circling ponies.

"Now what?" said Mr. Butler.

Tim was standing with his saddle swiveled under him, and Georgie was lying on the ground, moaning as if she was dying.

Caroline dismounted and gave Campbell's and Micky's reins to Tom. Camilla had jumped off Magpie and pulled his reins over his head so that she could help her sister. Phil leaned sideways and grabbed Tim's reins.

"Up you get," Caroline said encouragingly. "It was only a bump."

"My knee hurts," whined Georgie.

"Well, stand up and we'll see. Try not to let go of the reins another time."

Camilla helped her sister up, and we all watched as she flexed her leg and looked pained.

"How bad is it?" asked Mr. Butler. "If it's a real problem, you'll have to leave the trek to see a doctor. Can you walk?"

Georgie limped a few paces and nodded.

"Sure nothing feels too bad? We don't want you to continue if you'll make it worse."

"I'll be OK," she said.

"Good. Now, what happened here?"

"His saddle just slipped from under me," Georgie said. "I know I did the girth up properly. I always do."

"That's right. I saw her checking. It couldn't possibly have swiveled," her sister confirmed.

"Well, it clearly did. And you can see which notch it was buckled on – not the worn one. You must have made a mistake, Georgie."

"I didn't!" she insisted. "Someone else did it to make me fall."

"Don't be silly – who would do such a thing?" Caroline was dismissive as she sorted out Tim's saddle and gave Georgie a leg-up. "Everybody ready? Off we go again."

We rode along the ridge for ages, alternating trotting with walking. Megan and I stayed close together, chatting and laughing.

"Oh look, we've reached the end of the hills," she said suddenly.

Sure enough, there was a wide, steep escarpment that fell away in front of us. The hillside was dotted with trees and bushes, and the grass was rolling and uneven.

"Look!" called Phil. "Is it the sea?"

Water gleamed in the distance.

"It's a lake," said Mr. Butler. "A big one."

"Are we going there?"

"Can we swim?"

"Can we ride the ponies through it? I've always wanted to gallop through water."

"Yes, yes and yes," Mr. Butler answered, laughing. "But we've got to get down this hill first. You can spread out a bit and choose your own route. Don't let the ponies go too quickly, and remember to keep your weight steady – lean forward just a little to help them, but not so much that they're unbalanced. I'll lead Campbell and go the easiest way, on the diagonal, and Caroline will keep an eye on you all and follow behind. We'll stop for lunch at the bottom, by those bushes, see?"

Megan and I agreed we'd go more or less straight downhill, but slowly. Bilbo picked his way carefully, and I tried to stay as relaxed as possible, and to let my weight go with him as he swayed and jiggled. Megan had the reins just right, just tight enough to keep a contact with Star's mouth without tugging or unbalancing her, so I copied. The main thing seemed to be to grip tightly with your knees and lower legs. I could feel Bilbo's muscles as he switched angles, or as his foot sank unexpectedly deeper, and by the time we reached the valley floor, I felt far more in tune with him. I leaned forward to give him a good pat and ruffled his short mane, to say thank you.

All around us, the other ponies were picking their way carefully to the bottom of the hill. Mr. Butler had gone off to the right, where the slope was much shallower. Caroline was coming down alongside Georgie, offering her encouragement.

It was only when we were all assembled and dismounting, ready to untack the ponies for the lunchtime rest, that someone said, "Where are Tom and Phil?"

They were nowhere to be seen.

Chapter Seven

The hillside was empty. Nowhere in the wide expanse could we see two large boys on two larger ponies.

"Caroline – you were at the back?" said Mr. Butler.

"I was helping Georgie," she said, her voice worried. "I think I saw them go over there."

We all looked. The hillside broke up into folds of rock and bushes, but it didn't look possible for the boys to disappear.

"Everyone, yell," suggested Mr. Butler. "Now!"

"Tom! Phil!" Our shouts echoed weirdly off the hills, but there was no answering call.

"Something awful's happened," said Rosie in her voice of doom. "I can tell."

I felt a shiver of anticipation down my spine.

"Don't try to spook us," countered Megan. "They've probably just gone a bit farther than we can see."

"Quite right," said Caroline, matter-of-factly. "We'll just go and find them. It's not wise to get lost around here."

"Why not?" asked Emily, her eyes round. "Wild animals…?"

"There's only a few cows and sheep, silly. No, it's easy to get confused in this landscape. Once you've lost the route you're taking, you can lose your sense of direction. And there are some nasty drops…"

"We'll set up a search, but we'll stick together," said Mr. Butler. "Don't worry, they won't be far away. Emily and Rosie, why don't you stay here with Campbell? Then we can all see where to meet again."

They both said yes a little too quickly, and busied themselves with the three ponies. As we trotted away to the right, Megan whispered, "I bet they think there really are monsters here," and I whispered back "Maybe they're frightened of rabbits." We exchanged conspiratorial grins.

We soon got to where the landscape changed, and still there was no sign of the boys. The lake was now behind us, and hills closed in on both sides. A narrow valley wormed its way ahead, dotted with trees and outcroppings of rocks. To our right was the slope the boys might have tried to come down if they'd gone the way Caroline thought. It looked dangerously steep and treacherously rocky – but on the other hand there was no sign of the boys or their ponies, so there was no point in being melodramatic about what might have happened there.

"They're probably just around the corner," said Mr. Butler cheerfully. He split us up into four groups, Camilla and Georgie near the valley floor, Megan and I next, Mr. Butler higher up, and Caroline almost at the top.

"I don't see how they can possibly have disappeared," said Megan, guiding Star carefully through the tufted grass. "Where on earth could they go?"

It did look unlikely. But when I looked behind me I realized we'd already lost sight of Rosie and Emily. Looking up, Mr. Butler and the twins were still in view but Caroline was gone.

Within a few minutes, we'd reached a place where a stream had gouged out a twisting gully to our left.

"We'll explore up here!" Megan called to Camilla. She turned Star up the narrow streambed; there wasn't much room. "Come on, Jess. This is fun!"

It was. It was like plunging into a tunnel; the sun filtered just a little through the trees that were crammed close to the water. It was steep, and the ponies climbed slowly and carefully. Rocks studded the stream, creating little cascades and deep pools where the ponies tried to get their heads down to drink. I let Bilbo snatch a few mouthfuls. Then he saw Star was far ahead, broke into a half-trot, stumbled, and I nearly fell off. I clung on tightly, both feet out of the stirrups, my body halfway up his neck. I slithered back into the safety of the saddle with a feeling of a lucky escape. Fortunately, Bilbo decided to stop for more water, which gave me a chance to recover.

"Hurry up!" Megan called encouragingly, turning in the saddle. "This is great! It's like a lost world."

I pushed my feet back into the swinging stirrups, gathered the reins and kicked on. Bilbo shook his head, spraying me with water droplets, and clattered on uphill.

Annoying flies started to buzz around our heads. There were always flies around the ponies' heads, but usually they left us riders alone. Low branches meant that we had to duck all the time. On the other hand, there was a real feeling of adventure, and who knew? Maybe we'd find the boys before anyone else.

Finally, the valley widened into a little hollow, full of wild-flowers, backed by a miniature waterfall down a rocky cliff.

We let the ponies put their heads down. They drank thirstily.

"Well, Phil and Tom are not up here," I said.

It didn't look like anyone had ever been there before. The hollow was both beautiful and desolate. We couldn't see far in any direction; the hills had closed in around us, and there was nothing beyond them but blue sky. We could hear no sounds beyond the trickling of the waterfall and birdsong.

"Isn't it fantastic?" said Megan. She slid off Star and crouched down by the stream. She splashed water over her face and made a cup with her hands to drink.

"Isn't it dirty?" I asked, sliding off in turn and joining her. The water certainly looked inviting – it sparkled in the sun, and the waterfall was full of tiny rainbows that came and went like magic. The pool below was brownish and the water smelled a little strange.

"It's got peat in it, from the ground," said Megan. "My dad told me about it when we were on vacation last year. The peat makes the water look brown, but it's perfectly OK to drink. In fact, that's the water they use to make good whisky."

"Let's hope it makes us drunk, then," I said. I scooped up some drops and sipped. The strange smell was reflected in a strange, earthy taste, but it was refreshing and icy cold.

"Dad said it makes the bath water look really disgusting, as if someone's you know what-ed in it," said Megan.

We giggled and drank some more. I didn't know if I should say something to show I remembered that Megan's Dad had died. But what could I possibly say?

Bilbo jerked at his reins, which I'd looped over my arm. He wanted to cross to a patch of lush grass. I stood up and followed him. From there, I could see a glimpse of something gleaming in the far distance – maybe it was the lake. I wondered if Rosie and Emily were still winding themselves up with scary stories, and that reminded me that we were supposed to be looking for Tom and Phil.

"The others have probably found them by now," said Megan lazily, stretching out luxuriously next to the stream. Star fidgeted nearby and bent her head almost as if she was going to kiss her rider.

"Um, maybe we ought to get going. We don't want them setting up a search party for us."

"I suppose so." Megan scrambled to her feet and came over to me. "Wow, is that the lake? We've come miles."

"I think it must be. Should we start down?"

"We'd better. It makes you realize how easy it is to get lost up here, doesn't it? All this nothingness."

It certainly did. The boys could have gone practically anywhere. The hills were so deceptive. What looked open and clear was anything but.

Reluctant to leave, we remounted and set off downhill. The journey down wasn't so good. The ponies slithered a lot, and each time Bilbo skidded I held on even tighter and prayed I'd stay on. The overhead branches were harder to avoid going down and I got a painful scratch on my bare arm. Megan had a lucky escape when a twig poked her face but just missed her eye. The flies circled lazily, irritating the ponies and making them toss their heads unsettlingly. Then, when we got back to the valley floor, no one was around. I couldn't remember which way we'd come from, left or right.

Megan looked a bit worried, too.

"We went off to the left, didn't we?" she said.

"Did we?"

"Don't you remember, I called to Camilla from just here. At least..."

I shut my eyes and pictured the scene.

"No, the stream was opposite. On the right."

We dismounted again and stood holding the reins, turning in different directions and getting more and more confused. Coming along, it had seemed a straightforward valley floor, but now it had all sorts of angles and unexpected exits.

"I know, let's look for hoof prints," suggested Megan. "Hold on to Star so we don't get mixed up with new ones."

She examined the ground carefully, and quickly straightened up.

"Here are the tracks. Along this way and then up the stream."

Suddenly it all seemed easy and clear. We mounted and them stopped and looked at each other.

"Do we go on, or go back?"

"Back."

We turned the ponies and followed the double line of hoof prints. Before long, the valley opened up and in the distance we could see Rosie and Emily, looking around anxiously, while Twinkle, Mr. Man and Campbell grazed on the grass by their feet. They waved and we trotted back to them.

"Any news?"

"No. We went up a side route, and lost the others," explained Megan. "It's a lot easier to get lost here than you'd think."

We told them about our adventure.

"I've got such a bad vibe about all this," Rosie declared. "A premo – what do you call it?"

"A premonition? Maybe you're psychic," Emily encouraged her. She sounded impressed. "Concentrate and perhaps you'll 'see' the boys."

Rosie looked very solemn. "I can't see what's happened," she said, "but I'm sure it's something bad."

"Perhaps they've been bitten by poisonous snakes?" said Emily.

75

She and Emily were obviously winding themselves up to a state of delicious terror. I caught Megan's eye and she winked.

"We're a lot more likely to 'see' them if we go and look for them," she said, sarcastically. "How about you two go and we'll look after Campbell? Our ponies could use a rest."

"Mr. Butler told us to stay here," Emily said firmly.

Despite being worried about the boys, I wanted to laugh. Emily had no intention of putting herself into any danger, however imaginary.

"Well, do you want to come, Rosie, and I'll stay with Emily?" offered Megan, kindly. "Or the other way around?"

Emily stood close to Rosie and glowered at me. "We're fine here," she said.

"Off we go then," I said, putting Bilbo into a fast trot away from the two harbingers of doom.

Once out of their sight and hopefully their earshot, we stopped, convulsed in giggles.

"They're such a pair of wimps!" I sputtered.

"I know! They're just terrified of the big wide world," agreed Megan.

"I can 'see' they're in danger!" I intoned in imitation of Rosie.

"Scary!"

"Still, I suppose we'd better get back to business," I said, feeling serious again. "Because even though those two are being ridiculous, it's true that the boys are lost."

"This time, let's stick to the main valley till we catch up with the others," suggested Megan. "We can't possibly go wrong."

We went past the place where we'd gone up the little stream and rounded another corner. Suddenly, it was much more open again, and I could see Camilla a long way up the hill, holding Tim, Magpie and Captain in a bunch.

"Hey, where've you two been?" called Camilla, as we got nearer. She looked worried.

"Exploring," said Megan, briefly. "Have you found the boys?"

"Yes, but they're stuck. Look. Don't make too much noise."

We halted the ponies and slid off. She grabbed their reins and

76

we joined Georgie, who was lying on her stomach looking over the edge of a steep cliff.

The hill fell away sharply into what must once have been a quarry. The exposed earth was a mixture of sand and rocks, and there were almost no plants. A narrow path snaked down, almost vertically. Mr. Butler was scrambling carefully down it, holding on precariously to odd clumps of grass and protruding stones. Below, Phil and Tom were standing nervously while holding Bramble and Rolo. They were on a narrow ledge that faded away into nothingness almost immediately. The drop to the quarry floor wasn't far from there – just a couple of yards – but the ground was rough and unwelcoming. If the ponies moved suddenly, they could easily fall and seriously injure themselves.

Mr. Butler edged toward the boys. The ponies were facing away from him, and they would have to turn around to get back up the path.

"OK, don't do anything too quickly," he said, speaking softly and calmly. "Tom, take Rolo forward as far as you can."

Tom gathered Rolo's reins and pulled gently. The heavy gray pony moved obediently after him. A few bits of loose stone, dislodged by his hoofs, clattered ominously over the edge onto the quarry floor. We watched in silence, hardly breathing.

Mr. Butler squeezed past Bramble, who jiggled restlessly, setting up another shower of pebbles. Phil, looking pale, stroked Bramble's head steadily, keeping her under control as Mr. Butler came past.

"We can't turn them here," Mr. Butler muttered. We could only just hear him from our vantage point. "Tom, you can get down to the ground all right, can't you?"

"Easy. I can jump it."

"No, don't. We don't want to scare them into moving suddenly. And they can't go backwards. I'll get past Rolo somehow… yes, I've done it. Even if he is standing on my foot. OK, I'll hold him and you go on down along the path."

Tom nodded and passed the reins to Mr. Butler. It took him a while to find a possible route, and it was clearly too narrow and precarious for the ponies. Now he was on the quarry floor, we

77

were safely up above, and the ponies were still stuck with Mr. Butler and Phil halfway between.

"Now go and look for a way out," instructed Mr. Butler.

Tom nodded and disappeared. We all waited. The tension was horrible.

"If he doesn't find a way out, what will they do?" I whispered.

"I don't know. Maybe if they turned the ponies around, they could come back up?" said Megan.

"Um, but they can't get down that last section to turn them," said Georgie. "It's far too steep."

"What's happening?" called Camilla anxiously.

I scrambled up to tell her and offered to hold the ponies while she had a look. I didn't much want to watch any longer.

"Where's Caroline?" I said, suddenly realizing she was nowhere to be seen.

"She's gone to try to find another way into the quarry," Camilla said. "Don't let go of them, okay? I'm going to see if I can follow her."

Captain, Bilbo, Star, Magpie and Tim were standing patiently, as if they understood that this was a crisis and that they must behave. I looped the assorted reins over my arms and led them a bit further away from the edge, just in case one of them got any funny ideas.

There was a long pause while nothing happened. The sun was hot, and I felt strangely detached from all the drama. I pictured Rosie and Emily getting themselves all worked up, and wondered for a split second if maybe Rosie had really had a premonition. After all, the boys were in a very tight corner…

Then I pulled myself together. Nothing terrible was going to happen to the boys, and hopefully nothing to the ponies, either, now that Mr. Butler was in charge.

Megan came over to help me hold the ponies. I disentangled all the reins. "Any news?"

"Caroline's found a way into the quarry. She met Tom and they've come back to the bottom. Now they're going to try to widen the path so that the ponies can get down safely."

I ran over to the edge and lay down to look over. Tom and Caroline were scraping away madly at the ground to create a

78

walkway from the ledge. The earth was crumbly and came away in lumps, but gradually the path was looking more usable.

"OK, that should do it," said Mr. Butler. He spoke steadily, not wanting to scare the ponies. "I'm worried they'll skid badly or even try to jump down and hurt themselves. Caroline, stay at the end of the path and tempt them with something to eat."

Caroline balanced some pony nuts on her outstretched hand, and stood very still. Tom waited behind her. Camilla hovered in the background, holding Micky.

"Hold on to Bramble, Phil," instructed Mr. Butler. "I don't want her following yet. The ground's very unstable."

He had to lead Rolo from the front; the path was much too narrow for him to stay alongside. Rolo seemed to understand the danger he was in. He placed each heavy hoof with care and precision, plodding sensibly and slowly behind Mr. Butler. He was almost at the bottom when the path disintegrated under him. He floundered, all four legs splayed, but Mr. Butler pulled him forward quickly and Caroline encouraged him by showing the pony nuts. In a few seconds, Rolo was safely down on firm ground, burying his muzzle into Caroline's hand and being stroked by her and Tom.

Mr. Butler had already started uphill again.

Phil was looking very worried.

"She's so fidgety," he said. "I'm holding her as tightly as I can, but I can feel her trying to rush off."

Phil had one hand on Bramble's noseband while the other held the reins clasped tightly under her mouth. Even from where I was looking, I could see the tension in both of them. Bramble's dark body was darker still with patches of sweat. Mr. Butler crept up the steep slope carefully, so as not to alarm Bramble, but the pony skittered and chunks of earth broke away and clattered to the ground. Mr. Butler stopped.

"You'll have to bring her down, Phil," he said softly. "Just move in front and lead her gently."

Phil started to obey. He took a couple of tentative steps, but Bramble wouldn't move. Much more skitterish than Rolo, she'd decided she was in a dangerous place and her instinct was to do nothing.

"Let her see me," said Caroline. She'd pushed Rolo away and refilled her hand and was positioned at the bottom of the path. Mr. Butler went down quietly and waited beside her. Bramble stared down, as if she was wondering whether to risk moving for the sake of greed. Phil caressed her nose and pulled the reins gently, murmuring words of encouragement. For a long moment, nothing happened.

Then Georgie, next to me, yelled, "Ouch! That hurt!"

Chapter Eight

The result was amazing. Bramble reacted as if she'd been shot. She flung her head around toward us, wrenching the reins from Phil's grasp. Unbalanced by the sudden movement, her front legs slipped off the path and slid down the sheer rock. She shifted her weight onto her back legs for a second, rearing and looking for an instant like the statue of a warhorse. Her nostrils flared dramatically and her front hoofs flailed the air. Luckily, Phil reacted almost as fast and threw himself down the path, falling on top of Caroline. Almost in slow motion, Bramble gathered herself together, pushed off from her hind legs, and leapt into the air. A split second later, she was on the ground, shaking her head and trembling all over. Mr. Butler moved faster than I'd have thought possible and grabbed her trailing reins before she could trip over them. There was a scuffle of hoofs and flying mane and flashing eyes, and then everything went quiet.

At the foot of the path, Phil had catapulted Caroline to the ground. He got up quickly, flushing bright red, and held out a hand to help her up.

"I've just found out a good excuse not to lose weight," she said, rubbing her back. "And a good reason for wearing a hard hat. But next time you decide to fall off a cliff, tell me first, OK?"

Phil nodded and darted over to Mr. Butler and Bramble.

"Gently," warned Mr. Butler. "She's had enough of being scared for the moment." He soothed the frightened pony with little

81

murmurings and smooth caresses. Caroline joined him and they checked her legs and walked her around in a circle.

"She was lucky," said Mr. Butler. "No damage done. Are you OK to lead her, Phil?"

"Do you mind taking her till she's calmed down?" Phil asked. He'd obviously been really shaken by the whole affair. Mr. Butler nodded and soon a little procession wound its way out of our sight. The three of us – Megan had come as near as she could to watch, and the ponies had been no trouble – moved away from the quarry's edge and started downhill, and before long we met the others. They were emerging from a tangle of trees and bushes that masked the way into the quarry. Tom and Phil looked nervous. They must have been expecting a huge lecture, but so far nothing had happened.

"Everyone get on your ponies and we'll walk very quietly back to the lake," instructed Mr. Butler.

Phil looked hesitant, but when no one said anything to him he mounted Bramble and patted her gently. I watched surreptitiously as he gathered the reins and patted her sides carefully with his heels. She shivered momentarily, as if she was thinking of doing something drastic – bucking or bolting or throwing him off – and then her neck muscles softened and she moved into a slow, steady walk.

"Well done," said Mr. Butler, quietly, coming alongside on Captain. "Just keep her relaxed and soon she'll forget all about it."

Tom had jumped on Rolo – who seemed none the worse for his adventure – with his usual energy and was happily talking to Camilla. She was laughing at what he was saying. Georgie followed, sulking. I remembered her screech that had started off all the drama and wondered what had caused it, but I didn't think it was the right moment to say anything, so I concentrated on riding Bilbo properly and keeping him neatly in line. I didn't think it would exactly help matters if he chose this moment to bite another pony. Megan and Caroline brought up the rear, chatting cheerfully. Everything suddenly seemed normal again.

Rosie and Emily waved madly when they saw us coming, and seemed to have forgotten their dismal forebodings. Caroline said we could let the ponies roam as they would be hungry and thirsty and wouldn't go far, so we untacked them and they drifted off together towards the lake. It was way past lunchtime, and we were all starving, too. Luckily, there were slices of cheese, and packets of chips and fruit to eat – all instant and all filling. As we ate, we told Rosie and Emily what had happened. It sounded truly dramatic, and Megan made things sound even more exciting with the way she described our private adventure of following the stream up to the little glade, when really nothing had happened at all. Rosie seemed quite impressed at first, but then Emily made a disparaging comment about us. Rosie and Emily exchanged one of those sarcastic sort of looks that make you feel small.

Mr. Butler and Caroline sat on their own, talking earnestly.

"Have they said anything?" asked Camilla.

"Not a word," said Phil. "I hope they're not going to throw us off the trek." He looked miserable at the thought.

"They wouldn't!"

"They might. You did disobey orders," said Emily smugly.

"Don't be stupid. We're not in the army," I said impatiently. Rosie glared at me, and I felt a sudden pang of loss. Only two days ago, I'd thought Rosie and I were almost-best friends, and now everything she said was annoying me, and probably the other way around, too.

"What I don't understand is why you shrieked like that, Georgie," said Megan lazily, lying on her back and eating a banana. 'Was it your knee?"

"Jess hit me."

"What? I hit you? I didn't!"

Georgie turned red. "Well, something hit me. Like a needle going into me."

"And you thought it was me? Why didn't you say so at the time?"

"There was a lot going on ..." put in Camilla, looking embarrassed.

"True, but none of it was due to me," I protested.

"Could it have been a wasp?" asked Phil. "You ought to be careful if it was; lots of people are allergic to wasps."

"Well, Georgie obviously isn't," I said. "Or she wouldn't be OK now."

"That's not very nice, Jess," said Rosie. "It'd be awful to have an allergic reaction. You froth at the mouth and have to be rushed to hospital or you can die."

"Yes, but she isn't, is she?" said Tom. "Unless that's froth …' He leaned over in mock seriousness and gazed at Georgie's lips. "No, just potato chip crumbs."

Everybody except Georgie laughed and the subject was dropped. After a while, Mr. Butler called the boys over. They shambled over shamefaced, but came back a few minutes later looking cheerful.

"He said our behavior in a crisis was sensible enough for him to forgive us for making idiots of ourselves in the first place," reported Phil.

"So you're not off the trek?" asked Camilla, looking at Tom.

"Not off," he answered, grinning at her.

Phil plonked himself down between Megan and me. We went through the story again, laughing at the memories of Phil flattening Caroline and Bramble pretending to be a circus horse. Rosie and Emily wandered off down to the shores of the lake.

"Mr. Butler, can we swim?" called Tom.

"Haven't you caused enough trouble? You'd probably drown!" said Mr. Butler, joining us, looking perfectly cheerful.

"You did tell us to pack swimsuits," Camilla pointed out.

"True, and if it stays this warm, you can all swim a bit later. We're going to make our way around this lake to that area over there."

We all looked, shading our eyes against the sun.

"Why over there?" I asked.

"Two reasons. We're on a trek, so we should travel somewhere. But also, there's a farmhouse over there where we can use flushing toilets and get fresh water."

"Great!" said Megan. "Showers too?"

"Sorry, no. They're kind of old-fashioned and only have a bath, plus we couldn't expect them to produce enough hot water for ten of us."

"But you said we'd go swimming," said Tom.

"Exactly."

"So who needs a bath?"

"Girls do," answered Camilla. "We like to be clean, unlike you filthy boys."

"That's not true!" protested Phil. "I hate getting dirty."

"Yeah, well, maybe that says something about you," said Georgie. Phil turned red and didn't speak for a while. I hoped he wasn't going to start complaining. I liked him so much more this time.

"We left tonight's food at the farmhouse, too," added Caroline. "There was a limit to what we could expect Campbell to carry."

"Oh well, if there's food over there, let's get going," said Tom. "What sort of food?"

"Tom, you've only just had lunch! We'll be having a barbecue."

"Excellent."

Before long, we'd gathered the ponies, who had – sure enough – stayed close together, and were ready for the afternoon ride. I had a quick moment with Tim just before we set off, and told him how good he'd been when the ponies were waiting by the quarry. He snuffled comfortingly into my hand, and with my other hand I pulled his ears gently. I knew he liked that. Then Georgie came over and grabbed his reins without speaking to me, so I went back to Bilbo. As I mounted, I realized I'd gotten stiff and my arm was sore from yesterday, especially after scratching the same arm earlier. Bilbo didn't seem particularly energetic either. We found our place halfway along the line and walked along slowly. The steady swaying rhythm combined with the hot sun made me sleepy, and I had to pull myself upright in the saddle a couple of times. I let the reins hang loose and took my feet out of the stirrups so they could dangle freely. Rubber boots and a hard hat weren't ideal for a sweltering afternoon, especially when combined with sweat pants, and I wished we could ride in shorts and flip-flops.

The whole line had been lulled into a sleepy slowness. No one was talking, and the only sound was the muffled clop of the ponies' hoofs on the short grass and the twitter of birds high above us. Even the lake showed no movement.

Then Mr. Butler halted us, and we gathered in a circle.

"Anyone here ridden through water before?" he said. "Real water, not just a stream?"

86

"We have," said Camilla. "Last year on vacation. We stayed in a resort and rode white horses through the sea. It was totally amazing."

"Excellent," agreed Georgie. "Are we going to try that now?"

"Yes," said Caroline. "We'll trot down to the shore, and canter once we're there. Don't let the pace drop too much or the ponies will want to drink, and they really shouldn't while it's so hot out."

"Will Bramble be OK with this?" asked Phil.

Bramble was dancing about skittishly, and I remembered that at Easter she'd hated crossing water.

"She should be fine as long as she's with the others," said Caroline. "So keep up, and hopefully she won't even notice that we're in the water until we're there."

Phil sidled up next to me and we exchanged happy smiles. I'd always heard how much fun it was to gallop through water and now I was going to find out for myself. I felt much more confident about riding today. I'd remembered everything I'd learned at Easter and more. And I didn't even mind having Bilbo anymore. I was getting fond of his tough muscled black neck and his short brushy mane, and he'd whinnied in a friendly way to me when I'd caught him after lunch.

"Bilbo's OK in water, isn't he?" asked Phil.

"I think so. He's been fine so far."

We kicked into a trot and moved in a bunch down to the point where the lake water lay transparent over gravel and weeds. The second we entered it, a sharp spray of cool water was flung up over our hot bodies. It was blissful. Bramble trotted easily, not causing any problems.

"Everyone ready to canter?" called Mr. Butler, turning in the saddle to look at us all. There was a chorus of "Yes!" and within seconds we'd moved into a fast, splashy canter. It was fantastic. The spray sprinkled over our faces, the churned water glistened and gleamed all around us, and the ponies strained eagerly at their bits, asking to go faster. After a while, Mr. Butler let their pace extend so that we were going almost as fast as the previous day, but this time through sparkling, fountaining water.

We raced along the shore for ages, until there were rocks ahead and it wouldn't have been safe. Mr. Butler led us uphill out of the water, still at a canter, and then slowed to a sitting trot and quickly into a walk. Finally we stopped and slid off our ponies to thank them for such a wonderful ride. They tossed their heads and shook their ears, excited and exhilarated. We patted and stroked and caressed them.

Then Georgie said, " Oh, no! My saddlebag's fallen off."

"Did you seen where?"

She shook her head. "I was concentrating on the riding. I just noticed now. It's the one with all my makeup and everything in it." Her voice became a wail.

"Dear oh dear," said Mr. Butler. "You do seem to get all the bad luck, Georgie."

"Let's go back and find it," said Tom, leaping onto Rolo again and wheeling him around to face downhill.

"Not at a canter," warned Mr. Butler. "We need to let them all calm down. Yes, go with Georgie and see if you can find the bag, Tom. It can't be far."

I leaned happily against Bilbo's flank and watched. They trotted slowly back along our route and then Tom gave a shout. He leaned sideways but clearly couldn't reach down far enough, and then he did an amazing sort of twist and turned under Rolo's tummy and up the other side. He waved the lost saddlebag triumphantly.

"Wow, I wish I could do that," I said, enviously.

"Circus tricks," said Phil, but I sneaked a look at him and thought he'd like to do it too.

"Let's ask him to teach us," said Megan.

Georgie looked fed-up when she joined us.

"It's soaked," she complained, turning the bag upside down so that water dripped from it.

"It's all right," comforted Caroline. "You didn't bring any precious possessions with you, and everything will be dry soon. I'll loan you something to wear if you need it."

We all stifled giggles at the thought of Georgie wearing anything of Caroline's. Georgie was on the large side, but she wasn't even half Caroline's size, Still, it was a nice gesture.

"Make sure it's attached firmly this time," said Mr. Butler, looking rather impatient.

'It wasn't me...' Georgie started, but Captain was clattering off and Mr. Butler didn't pay any attention. Georgie pushed Tim past Megan and me and maneuvered herself next to Emily. They talked solidly for the next hour or so, while we walked the ponies around the lake. Eventually we saw in front of us the farmhouse that Mr. Butler had pointed out earlier. It looked as if it had been there, tucked in a sheltered corner of the lake, protected from heavy weather by folded hills and little groups of trees, for as long as the lake itself. A few sheep were pastured in a field alongside the house, and some black and white cows in another field. Other than that, there wasn't much sign of life, and certainly not much sign of civilization. It all looked gorgeous in the summer sun, but I couldn't help thinking that on a cold, wet February day it might have been the most desolate, unfriendly spot ever. Maybe there was something to be said for town life after all. But for now, it was a perfect setting.

The farmer came out to meet us, and said we should turn the ponies out with the sheep. I'd have thought he'd be glad to see us, as he was all alone and miles from anywhere, but he looked as if he'd had his expression permanently stuck on "gloom." He didn't smile at all, and his voice was monotonous and sounded tired.

"What's up with him?" I asked Caroline as we led Bilbo and Micky through the field entrance.

"Nothing, he's always like this."

"How depressing for his family!"

"I don't think he's got one. He's always alone whenever I've been up here."

I shivered. "It can't be much fun in the winter," I said.

"You're right. It's pretty cold up here in the hills in January and February, and being all alone must be horrible."

"Still, you'd think he'd be glad to have our company," I persisted.

Caroline laughed. "Not him. He'll be glad of the bit of money we give him for the camping space and all that, but he's not very sociable. Some people are like that, you know."

She let Micky go and went over to one of the others. Bilbo tugged at the halter rope, so I gave him a quick pat and let him go, too. He trotted away a few yards, and then put his head down to the grass.

I wandered back to where we'd left our gear, wondering about how someone could choose to live all alone and not want any friends. I just couldn't imagine being like that. All around me, my friends were untacking ponies, starting to put up tents, giggling, squabbling gently, and gossiping. How could anyone want to miss out on that?

"As soon as you're set up, you can go for a swim!" yelled Mr. Butler.

Megan and I got that tent up faster than you'd believe possible. We flung our saddlebags inside, rummaged in them for swimsuits, changed in a flurry of elbows and legs, grabbed our towels, and sprinted down to the water's edge.

We stopped there. There were half a dozen swans floating in the lake, an arm's length away. They were staring at us as if we were from outer space. Actually, I suppose we might as well have been, if you spent your life in that lake. But I couldn't help remembering tales of swans attacking people and even breaking arms with a single vicious swipe of their white-feathered wings, and I certainly didn't want to be the first one in.

Camilla joined us. I'd expected her to be wearing a stylish bikini but she had on a plain black swimsuit. My scarlet and gray one felt glamorous in comparison.

She said, "What are we waiting for?"

"Well ... " Megan and I said in unison, pointing to the swans, who gazed back impassively.

"They won't hurt us," she said confidently, and waded in. The water was over her knees almost at once. The swans paddled away nonchalantly and I felt silly to have worried about them.

We all watched as Camilla took a couple more steps, and then dived in neatly. Her sleek body sliced through the water. She turned onto her back, waved and called, "Come on, it's cool."

"I bet it is," grumbled Phil, edging gingerly in and shivering dramatically.

"Don't be a wimp," said Megan, running past him. "Come on, Jess!"

I felt a bit like Phil, but I wasn't going to show it. The water felt freezing to start with, but as soon as I started swimming, it warmed up and had a lovely, silky smoothness, quite different from the sea or a swimming pool. Before long, we were all swimming, splashing and fooling around. The lake was the perfect depth – all of us could stand up, just, and yet it was deep enough to play diving games and attack people under water. Tom and Camilla kept chasing and dunking each other, and laughing when their mouths weren't full of water. Then Caroline plowed in and brought in a ball, which we used for a game of dodgeball with Tom and Phil in the middle. It was a blast.

Later, we sat around the campfire and helped cook massive quantities of hot dogs and burgers. My skin felt as if it was glowing – first from the sun all day, then from the exercise and now from the fire.

"I'm not burned, am I?" I asked Megan, twisting to try to see the back of my arms. "You're lucky. I wish I was as dark as you."

"I have to moisturize, though," said Megan, "and my tan doesn't really show."

"Mine does," said Rosie. "I go red. That's why I keep putting on sunscreen."

It was true, she'd definitely gotten burned. Caroline inspected Rosie's skin and said she'd have to be extra careful tomorrow.

"What about me?" asked Phil. "D'you mind checking, Jess?"

I got up and stood behind him, checking his neck for redness. "You're OK," I said. Then I noticed how close I was to him, and that all the others were watching us, and I turned bright red myself. I sat down quickly between Megan and Emily. Phil smiled across to me and I smiled back involuntarily, and then busied myself with chopping carrots for the salad.

We ate a huge meal and sat around afterwards telling stories and making jokes. Camilla told a long and complicated ghost story as the shadows grew, and really spooked us. Somehow, I'd ended up next to Phil, and I couldn't help grabbing his arm for a second when Camilla reached the terrifying climax of her story. Later I felt his arm sort of resting against my shoulders. It felt friendly and warm, and I snuggled back against it and felt very happy.

91

"Where's Georgie?" asked Caroline suddenly.

"She's probably gone to the bathroom, now that we've got a real one," said Rosie. "I'll go and see."

Emily decided – inevitably – that she needed to go too so the group broke up. Phil and I wandered over to the pony paddock. The ponies were almost invisible now except for the grays – Rolo and Tim – but you could still just pick out the sheep scattered across the grass.

"Isn't this great?" I said.

"Fantastic," Phil replied.

I thought for a moment he was going to lean forward and kiss my cheek, and I really wouldn't have minded. But there was a sudden flurry of movement and Georgie appeared out of the shadows.

"Hi. Where've you been?" I asked casually.

She glared at me.

"None of your business," she snapped.

"Sorry."

"Been busy talking to Tim?" she inquired nastily.

"Well, no. To each other."

She tossed her head and went over to the campfire. Emily and Rosie had come back from the house and asked where she'd been, too, but she wasn't saying. Another mystery, I thought, like the saddle and the shriek, but not worth worrying about.

"Time for bed, everyone," called Mr. Butler. "Another long day tomorrow."

We all said good night and crawled into our tents.

"What's up with Georgie?" whispered Megan, once we'd gotten settled.

I tried and failed to find a soft spot to lie on and thought for a moment.

"I really don't know," I said. "But every time I get near Tim, she stresses out."

"Camilla's OK, though."

"Yes, and I didn't think I'd like her at all at first."

"I thought she was a snob."

"Me too."

93

"It just shows how easily you can be wrong. D'you think she and Tom like each other?"

I thought back over the day. "Mmm-hmm. Lucky her. He's so good-looking."

"Phil's not so bad," she said slyly, and we both giggled.

"No more talking!" called Mr. Butler from outside. Through our open tent entrance, we could see shadows moving as he and Caroline cleaned up and made the fire safe. Further away, we could hear ponies moving restlessly, stamping a foot or snorting, and beyond again an owl hooted eerily.

Then I was asleep.

Chapter Nine

We slept longer that night. The sun wasn't pointed straight at our tent opening so it didn't wake us up, but when I finally surfaced from deep, happy pony dreams, the whole tent glowed and felt warm and slightly stuffy. Megan must have woken during the night and zipped us in. I lay idly, half-reading the book I'd brought and lazily watching the shadows of leaves flickering over the tent walls. There were voices outside, not too near, and the sound of birds twittering away, along with the smell of coffee brewing.

Megan opened her eyes and saw that I was awake.

"OK?" she murmured sleepily.

"Great."

She struggled up into a sitting position. "Are you sure? I've been worrying that I've somehow broken up your friendship with Rosie."

No, I thought, that wasn't you. That was Emily.

"Don't worry about it," I said out loud. "I haven't been friends with her for that long. If she likes someone else better, it's no skin off my nose. Anyway, you and I have made friends with each other instead."

"True," Megan said solemnly and then she laughed. "Rosie's missed out on a lot of fun being with Emily, anyway. That girl's always making a big deal about nothing."

"They probably didn't sleep at all last night after Camilla's ghost story," I added, remembering how they'd clutched each other in mock – or not so mock – terror at all the scary parts.

95

"Camilla's fun," said Megan, thoughtfully, "but Georgie's a bit weird. Always getting herself into trouble."

"Yes, and then there was last night." I told Megan about how Georgie had appeared out of nowhere and snapped off Phil's and my heads for nothing.

"Maybe it's something to do with being a twin," mused Megan. "You should know, Jess, you've got twins."

"They're not really big enough yet to be proper twins," I said, "and they're not identical; I'm sure that makes a difference. They're just like an ordinary brother and sister who happen to be the same age. Poor Mom and Dad – they'll have been up for hours by now, and all stuck together in an RV with no escape."

My Mom's on her own this week." Megan's voice went very sad. "Ethan and Jamie are at a football camp."

I went hot with shame. How could I go on about my parents without remembering that Megan's dad had died?

"Do you want to phone her?" I asked. "I know there's the rule, but I'm sure..."

"No, it's OK," she said, brushing away a tear that was running down her cheek as if she hadn't even noticed before that she was crying. "I said I could call tonight from the farm, but Mom said she'd be OK on her own. She doesn't like me making a big deal over her."

I thought about what it would be like to lose a parent, and especially a father. My dad could be incredibly annoying and insensitive, but I couldn't bear to be without him. And it sounded as if Megan had to deal with her mother's grief as much as with her own. I put a comforting hand on her shoulder and she stayed still for a moment as if it might be helping, and then said, "Time to get up. I'm starving."

I leaned forward and unzipped the tent. The campfire was burning cheerfully and Caroline was just starting to cook bacon. The smell was amazing.

"Get ready and you can help," she said.

We ran to the farmhouse and used the bathroom – which normally I'd have hated, as it was old-fashioned and a bit smelly, but after two days of fields it was absolutely blissful. Then we came back and got dressed in T-shirts and shorts. It was too hot for pants. I took over the frying pan, which was crammed with bacon. I had to balance it on the little grill we'd brought with us and jiggle the slices around so they wouldn't burn. Meanwhile, Megan was setting out cartons of orange juice and mugs for coffee for the older crowd. That freed Caroline to go around to the other tents, waking everyone up. There were a lot of moans and groans, but once they'd all dragged themselves out of their sleeping bags and had smelled the food, no one seemed too resentful.

"Where's Mr. Butler?" asked Tom through a mouthful of bread and bacon. He'd managed to wriggle from his tent to the campfire without leaving his sleeping bag, and just his arms and head stuck out from its cozy depths.

"Over there."

We followed Caroline's pointing finger and way up high above the farm. Mr. Butler and the farmer were moving around in a field.

"What are they doing?" asked Phil.

"Getting the jumps ready."

Jumps! There was a general feeling of excitement and anticipation as we all swallowed our breakfasts and did the chores that Caro-line assigned to us. People were sort of buzzing with knowing they'd be jumping. I wasn't so sure. I'd only done the most basic jumping at Easter – well, not really even that, just trotting over a line of poles – and I wasn't at all sure about starting to do it for real. Still, I comforted myself, Mr. Butler knows that, and he's always shown me what to do before. He'll probably do the same again.

Once everything was packed, and left in a big pile to load onto the ponies later, we were told to gather the ponies and groom them. Bilbo seemed quite pleased to see me and whiffled softly against my arm as I brushed out his coat.

That didn't take too long, and then we started tacking up. Mr. Butler had joined us and was wandering around inspecting ponies for missed bits of grooming. He was telling people off like he always did. I didn't mind – it was part of being on the trek. Rosie, Georgie and Emily seemed to have made a three-some, which left Meagan and me mostly alone, but sometimes

97

with Phil, who was behaving shyly for some reason. Camilla and Tom were together a lot, giggling and joking and looking very pleased with themselves.

"You'd better change out of those shorts, you two," said Mr. Butler, from behind us.

I looked around from the complicated task of adjusting Bilbo's throat lash, the piece of the bridle that goes from the brow band under his neck. I was worried that it was too tight, especially in such hot weather.

"Do we really have to?" asked Megan. "It's so hot …"

"You'll regret it if you don't," warned Caroline, one thigh balanced in the air as she adjusted her stirrup leathers. "Your legs'll be rubbed raw."

"She's right," put in Camilla. "We did a long ride last year and wore shorts, and it was a disaster. I swore never again. That's why I stick to jodhpurs now."

"Yeah, well, I would if I could," I said, goaded, "Except they're too expensive for some of us."

"Hey, I didn't mean anything. Keep your shirt on."

Camilla flapped the air as if there was a fire burning between us and that made me laugh.

"Sorry," I muttered. "That was silly of me."

"It's OK. I just wish we had ordinary T-shirts with us. For some reason, Georgie and I only brought long-sleeved shirts, and it's boiling today."

"Would you like to borrow one?" I suggested. "It's clean…"

"That'd be great."

I dug out the extra T-shirt I'd packed the first evening, when everyone else was sticking in makeup and hair straighteners and things like that; things they'd long since forgotten. Well, not entirely forgotten – Rosie and Emily had both managed to put on full makeup both days. Camilla stripped off her shirt and quickly substituted the T-shirt.

"Thanks', she said, "and sorry if I upset you. I forgot you didn't have jodhpurs. Those pants are fine, though."

"A bit hot," I said, pulling them on reluctantly instead of my nice, cool shorts, "but that's life."

98

We didn't say anything else, but I felt a warm feeling of friendship. We all swung onto our ponies easily; two days of mounting and dismounting, to say nothing of the hours of riding in between, were doing great things for my level of fitness. I couldn't imagine how Caroline managed to stay so heavy when she rode so much.

Bilbo tossed his head and took a few steps as I collected the reins and sorted out the stirrups. Instinctively, I tightened my grip and turned him, taking control and bringing him back to a halt. As I wriggled into a comfortable position in the saddle, I felt sure of myself. I was a real rider now.

Mr. Butler led us along in a cheerful, chattering group. We passed through several fields till we reached the far one where the farmer was lounging against the field gate, watching us pass. He gave Bilbo a hefty, unexpected slap on the flank as we went by. Bilbo reacted, understandably enough, by skittering into a short uncontrolled canter. He barged into Rolo and then into Tim. Tom saw me coming and gathered Rolo together quickly, but Georgie was talking to Emily. As Tim lurched to one side, she went with him, but while Tim regained his balance Georgie didn't. She flew off sideways so that she was hanging on with one leg in the stirrup and the other on the top of the saddle, her fingers grabbing for the saddle pommel and slipping off the smooth leather. There was a moment of suspended animation, when she hung impossibly off Tim's side. Then she plopped neatly onto the grass, unfortunately just where Bramble had deposited a large, smelly, steaming pile of poop.

Georgie sat there open-mouthed in horror. Camilla and Megan jumped off their ponies and took an elbow each to pull her up. Her back and both her hands were covered in the stuff and her face was scarlet with anger and mortification.

She yelled a series of names at me that I won't record. I felt just awful. I hadn't done it on purpose, but how could I make her understand that? To make matters worse, everyone else gathered around in a big circle watching us – I'd dismounted and Bilbo was standing just behind me as I faced her, with Camilla and Megan on either side sort of supporting her at arms' length. I couldn't think what to say except for "Sorry" so that's what I did.

"That's enough." Mr. Butler stood between us and mercifully partly hid Georgie from my sight. "It's not the end of the world, Georgie, just an unfortunate accident. Let's get you cleaned up."

"But these jodhpurs cost a ton!" she wailed.

More the fool you are for wearing them then, I thought, and I imagine most of the others thought that too. A ripple of laughter started, and I had to concentrate really hard to control myself. She looked so funny, covered in muck and furious. Then I remembered when Mike had pushed me into a muckheap at Easter and how I'd hated it. That sobered me.

"Come on. We'll find you something to wear," said Caroline.

"But none of us has any spare clothes!" whined Georgie.

"You can have my jodhpurs," offered Camilla, "and my shirt. I wasn't wearing it anyway."

"Yes, but you'll need some pants yourself. Does anyone have any?"

After a minute I said, "If Camilla doesn't mind wearing my sweat pants, I'll wear shorts. It was sort of my fault since Bilbo started it."

I hoped the farmer would say, no, it was actually his fault, but he seemed to be a man of few words. He also obviously thought the whole thing was very funny.

"That's very kind of you, Jess," said Mr. Butler. "You'll probably get a bit sore, but it can't be helped. But wouldn't it be easier if you passed your pants straight over to Georgie?"

No one actually said anything, but the glare that Georgie gave me was probably explanation enough. We left the ponies in the care of the others and followed Caroline back down through all the fields to where we'd camped. I dug out my shorts and took off my sweats for Camilla. She in turn changed from her jodhpurs.

"Will they fit you?" asked Caroline doubtfully.

Georgie glared again. "We are identical twins," she stated.

"Yes, but..."

Georgie grabbed the jodhpurs and a couple of towels and marched off to the farmhouse. Caroline said something about running her a bath and followed her. Camilla, now wearing both my T-shirt and my sweats, gave me a conspiratorial look.

We waited till they were out of earshot.

"Oh, Camilla, I'm so sorry," I said. "I promise I didn't do it on purpose. It was that horrible farmer who hit Bilbo."

"I know, I was just behind you," said Camilla. "And I think you've been really nice about it. Don't worry about Georgie. She'll be OK. And thanks for the clothes."

"You look great in them," I said, and she laughed.

"Let's hope Tom agrees."

She went off to the farmhouse. I hung around and then thought I might as well go back to the others. I tramped up through the fields, passing the farmer on his way down. He grinned at me as if it was all a big joke and I felt like telling him it wasn't for me, but he slapped me on the back and went on. When I joined the others, Rosie trotted over on Twinkle and said sarcastically,

"At least the farmer seems to approve of what you did, Jess." And she turned her back on me very obviously.

I didn't get the time to find out what that was all about. Mr. Butler called me over to join in, so I collected Bilbo from where he'd been tied up and walked him steadily to the middle of the field to see what had been assembled for us to jump over.

There were four jumps in all, arranged in a big circle. The nearest one was a long thin tree trunk that was lying on the grass. That was more or less what I'd jumped before. Then there was a further pole balanced at either end of two straw bales. It wasn't far off the ground, but there was a definite gap between the ground and the pole. I felt a flutter of butterflies at the thought of asking Bilbo to lift off enough to clear it. The third jump was a similar height, but made entirely of straw bales, which somehow looked less daunting. Then the final one was a pole that rested on two oil drums; it was about twice the height of the others and way more than I had any intention of trying.

Camilla appeared, panting slightly after running uphill. As she got on Magpie, she reported that Georgie was nearly cleaned up and that she and Caroline would join us shortly.

"About time too," said Mr. Butler, who I suspect thought making a fuss about sitting in a pile of poop fairly unnecessary. "Now then, a reminder about jumping for those of you who're used to it and some information for those of you who aren't." He smiled across to me and I felt much safer at once. "What you've got to remember first is that these aren't riding school ponies who've been schooled at jumping and do it most days. These are good-quality, brave and experienced trekking ponies. They've all done a bit of jumping at one time or another, but none of them's an expert. So don't expect too much from them."

We all nodded and patted our ordinary, lovely ponies, who shuffled and flicked ears and swished tails in their ordinary, lovely way.

"Shorten your stirrups by a couple of holes," Mr. Butler instruct-ed. We all did. "Now walk round in a big circle."

We guided the ponies into a line. They followed each other contentedly. We had to practice what Mr. Butler called, "Jumping Position." That meant leaning forward but keeping our legs parallel to the girth. That sounds simple, but it was surprisingly hard to get exactly right. Tom insisted on leaning so far forward that his head was in Rolo's mane and his bottom way out of the saddle.

"I'm only doing like jockeys do!" he protested.

"Fair enough, but if Rolo stumbles you'll come off," warned Mr. Butler.

We were just about to start actually jumping when Caroline and Georgie came back. It looked as if her sister's jodhpurs really were too tight for Georgie. She also looked as if she didn't ever want to see me again. So what, I thought. I hadn't done anything wrong and I'd said sorry when it wasn't really Bilbo's or my fault at all.

I was also really enjoying wearing shorts, even if they did look a little odd with boots. I was so much cooler and more comfortable.

Georgie and Tim joined the circle as far away from me as they could, and Mr. Butler ran through the instructions again for her benefit, although at the end she said, "Don't worry, we jump all the time at home." I'd have expected a sarcastic remark from Mr. Butler at that, but maybe he felt sorry for her; anyway, he just told Tom to lead into the first jump and then to circle back around at a trot.

The line went into a neat sitting trot, and Tom led the way over

102

the pole on the ground. We popped over it in succession, and there was no time to feel nervous. It was really easy.

We did that a couple of times, and then Mr. Butler told Tom to include the second jump.

"Can we canter?" he asked.

"Not yet. You only need to canter for impetus and this is still very low."

So we followed around, still at a sitting trot, and after the pole we came up to the pole on top of the bales. Again Bilbo took off without me doing anything and we were over. There was a definite feeling of lifting off the ground this time, and I could see why we needed to lean forward, as otherwise you could feel left behind.

We did that a couple more times and then stopped for a rest. Bilbo tossed his head about temperamentally, excited. I held on tightly and wondered, a bit nervously, about the last two jumps. I also noticed that I was getting a little sore already along the side of my legs, especially where I'd been gripping hard. Georgie saw me rubbing the sore patch and looked pleased, so I stopped.

"We're not counting strides, are we?" asked Emily.

"I am," said Phil.

I wasn't exactly sure what they meant, but Caroline explained.

"Ideally, you should work out the best place for your pony to take off, and then make sure he takes the right number of strides to be in the perfect place for takeoff," she said. "In a practice field like this, there's lots of leeway, but in a real competition, if you get the number of strides wrong, your pony will probably refuse to jump or make a mess of it."

"But how do you work that out?" asked Rosie.

"It's down to experience, basically. You learn to judge the length of your pony's stride, and in a competition you can measure distances by walking the course."

"We're doing a competition on Saturday, but I'll never be able to do that," I said, alarmed.

"Don't worry, you won't have to. It's a very informal horse show and gymkhana. The jumping class you're all entered for is very basic."

"What a pity," muttered Camilla, but she didn't say it loud enough for others to hear.

We started off again. This time we went faster, but we still trotted rather than cantered. Bilbo nipped over the first pole, pushed off and cleared the second one, and then trailed his feet in the last one and took half a straw bale with us down the field.

"I know we said you don't have to count strides, but give him a little incentive, Jess," called Mr. Butler. "Kick just before takeoff and he won't trail his back legs."

I nodded, feeling silly. I hadn't been doing any kicking or even squeezing. Bilbo had happily done the whole course by himself.

We went around one more time, but this time I pushed my heels against Bilbo's sides as we approached each obstacle. On the last one he leapt miles into the air and landed with a thump that nearly shook me off.

"That's better," said Mr. Butler approvingly. "Don't overdo it, though."

I was just about to say something when he added, "OK, last time and this time all four jumps. Away you go."

I was taken completely by surprise. Bilbo followed the others enthusiastically, and I felt as if I was about a yard behind him. Every time he rose in the air I was struggling to keep up – or on – and when we turned towards the big jump I was so busy trying to keep hold of the reins and keep my feet in the stirrups that I didn't even notice the jump.

"Well done, everyone," said Mr. Butler, as we assembled in front of him. "We'll do more jumping tomorrow – lots of it – but this was a useful start. OK, Jess?"

"I think so," I gasped, still flustered. "I sort of lost control at the end there."

"Don't worry, Bilbo knows what he's doing. You've got a good pony there. Right, everyone off, lead the ponies down to the camping area. We'll have some lunch, and then we'll trek back to the farm."

I slipped off Bilbo and pulled the reins over his head to lead him. He plodded along behind me down through the fields again. At the bottom I untacked him before turning him out for a brief rest.

"Mr. Butler's right, you're a great pony," I said lovingly to him as I slipped the bridle over his head and pulled the bit gently from his mouth. "I'm sorry I wasn't happy to have you at the start."

And would you believe it, he chose that exact moment to bite my arm.

Chapter Ten

The rest of that day was uneventful. We mostly walked the ponies, along quiet tracks and through woods with welcome shade. We went along the side of a big wheat field where we leaned sideways to pick the ripe grain and nibble it. It was hard to stop the ponies from stuffing themselves silly. The heat was stifling, and no one felt energetic. In fact, I felt a little queasy most of the time, and I don't think I was the only one. Flies were everywhere, tormenting the ponies by swarming around their eyes and buzzing irritatingly around our faces. The long line of riders and ponies was characterized by flicking hands and tails, as we all, ponies and humans alike, fought off the flies.

It was almost dusk when we reached the familiar farmhouse where the pony vacations were based. We trailed tiredly into the stable yard and slid off the ponies. Mr. Butler looked around at us.

"I know you've all had enough, but you know what I'm going to say, don't you?"

"Ponies before people," we chorused. He grinned cheerfully.

"Absolutely right, but don't worry, a quick rub over with a dandy brush'll be fine tonight. Check their feet like you always do, and hang the tack up carefully; it got damp last night so you need to take care of it tonight."

We worked in a sort of daze, untacking, brushing ponies, washing and checking hoofs for stones lodged in the iron shoes. When I was finally finished, I led Bilbo by his halter rope down to the paddock. I hadn't been feeling quite so thrilled with him after the bite he'd given me, but now he pushed his nose into my stomach and breathed heavily and affectionately. I pulled and stroked his ears and forelock and forgave him.

Phil came by, leading Bramble, and laughed at us.

"You look like one of those man and beast things, a centaur," he said. "You know, the body of a horse and the head of a man."

"Except this is a pony and a girl," I said, giving Bilbo one last stroke and pushing him away.

"Very true," said Phil. "I'd noticed you're a girl, actually."

He took my hand; his was warm and dry and I felt very happy with life all of a sudden. Bilbo suddenly turned and cantered away, and Bramble followed as if they were playing tag.

"How come they're not tired and we're exhausted?" I mused as we strolled back to the farmhouse.

"It's because we do everything for them," Phil said. "We make all the decisions."

"Bilbo makes most of the decisions where I'm concerned," I said, but I was laughing.

There was time for a shower before supper. Even though we'd been swimming, I felt really dirty and loved standing under the stream of steaming water, washing my hair properly and afterwards smothering myself with the body lotion that Megan had loaned me. The bruise from the first day's fall was dramatically purple and you could see where Bilbo had nipped me each time, too. But I'd also gotten a great tan.

All of us girls decided to put on our pajamas for supper and have a cozy time in our rooms afterwards. Phil looked disappointed when we came downstairs and told him and Tom, but although I was really enjoying being with him, I didn't want to start spending too much time together. I wanted to make sure I was friendly with everyone and anyway, a bit of girlie pampering seemed definitely in order.

So after stuffing ourselves with roast chicken and fries and peas, we left the boys watching football on television and all gathered in our room, which was the biggest. We tried on each other's makeup. Rosie produced her hair straighteners, which she'd carted

107

unnecessarily on the trek, and let the rest of us try them. Emily's brown hair was straight anyway but she still tried them first. My hair's shoulder length and a little wavy and it doesn't suit me straight, but Camilla's long blond beautifully cut hair looked even better when it was sleek and shiny. Georgie's hair was just the same, but somehow the treatment didn't work so well for her. Perhaps it was because her hair was more oily. I felt sorry for her and told her she looked great, but she ignored me. Megan's hair, of course, was black and curly, and she said there was no point in even trying. She had some cool makeup, though, in different shades from mine, and lots of smelly things, like the body lotion and some spray perfume that we all used.

Mrs. Butler knocked on the door and came in with drinks and cookies about ten o'clock, which was kind of her. She laughed at us, a bit unfairly, I thought. Mind you, Rosie was squeezing herself into Camilla's tight jeans at the time, so maybe that's what was so funny.

Rosie and Emily and Georgie were distant towards me all evening, but I stayed near Camilla and Megan and it didn't bother me. When we decided we really couldn't keep awake any longer, at about midnight, Megan invited me to move into her room rather than stay with Rosie and Emily.

"Do you mind, Rosie?" I asked, feeling a bit embarrassed even though we hadn't been getting along.

"Go ahead. Em and I can gossip," she said, in an offhand way.

I wondered if that meant they'd gossip about me, but I grabbed my stuff and hefted it across the corridor to Megan's room, which was nicer than ours anyway as it had a view over the pony paddock. Not now, of course – it was pitch black – but it would be great in the morning.

Camilla and Georgie were next door and as we scrambled into bed I thought I could hear raised voices, as if they were arguing. But I was too tired to worry about anything. I let my eyes close, and the next thing I knew it was daylight. Megan was leaning out of the window trying to entice the swallows that swooped everywhere to come and take cookie crumbs from her hand.

"It might work with pigeons," I said, joining her sleepily. "But I don't think swallows ever stop flying."

"They must stop to sleep," she said, logically, "and to have babies. Have you seen their nest?"

I leaned out and looked upwards at the underside of the roof. A mess of straw, clay and grass seemed to be stuck to the tiles.

"Is that their nest?"

"Sure. If we'd been here in the early summer we'd have seen them swooping in to feed their babies. They'll be thinking about migrating south soon, though."

It seemed impossible that the summer would ever end. It had been hot for weeks, and taking coats and sweaters on the trek had been a waste of time, but Megan said, "I wouldn't be surprised if we had rain later. Look at the clouds over in the distance."

The clouds didn't look like much to me, but she was proven right soon enough. We got dressed in jeans and T-shirts and took the dirty things from the trek down with us to be washed. When we went out into the yard after breakfast the clouds had filled the sky. Everything had become dull and gloomy, and a few splashes of rain warned of more to come.

We'd been told to clean tack first, so we gathered in the tack room and polished leather and metal for an hour or so. Phil and Tom came over to Camilla and me and told us about the football game in excruciating detail. They must have described every single play. It was nice being with them, and I felt proud of having a sort-of boyfriend when most of the others didn't, but they were incredibly boring.

Everyone was feeling tired and crabby. Rosie and Emily bickered over which bridle was which, and Camilla and Georgie hardly spoke to each other. Then a flash followed by an ear-splitting crash broke our lethargy. Everyone jumped and dropped things. A second flash followed almost instantly, along with an even louder drumroll of thunder. We crowded to the window to look outside. The sky had turned almost black. As we watched it was split again by a terrific lightning flash. Again the thunderclap was instantaneous.

"I hate storms," whispered Rosie, looking very pale. I put a comforting arm around her without thinking, but Emily pulled her away and glared at me.

"I love them," announced Tom. "Just look at that!"

The sky split and crashed again.

"It must be right overhead," said Camilla. "There's no gap at all between the thunder and lightning."

"Something awful will happen," moaned Rosie.

"Predicting the future again, Rosie?" said Megan sarcastically.

I realized this was almost word-for-word a rerun of the dire predictions Rosie had made two days earlier. I wanted to giggle.

"We'll get struck. I know we will," insisted Rosie, looking furious.

"Not if we don't go running around in it," pointed out Camilla.

Phil took my hand. "You OK, Jess?"

I shook him off impatiently. "Of course I am. It's only a storm."

Maybe that wasn't the right thing to say. He tightened his lips and looked away. Oh brother, I thought, was I supposed to pretend to be silly and girlie just to make him feel protective?

Mr. Butler sprinted across the yard – a raincoat spread over his head and flying behind him in the wind like wings – to check on us.

"How long will it last?" asked Georgie.

"Hard to say. We've been building up to this storm for days, so it'll be best if it's a big one. Otherwise it'll hang around and spoil things."

"Are the ponies all right?" I asked, suddenly worried about them out in the storm.

"They'll be fine. They're country ponies, used to being outdoors in all weather. They'll appreciate a good grooming after all this blows over, though."

As he spoke, the heavens opened and rain poured down in torrents. In seconds, the dry stable yard floor was inches deep in water, which swirled up to the bottom of the tack room door.

"Are we going riding this morning?" asked Emily.

Mr. Butler looked at her for a moment, as if she was particularly stupid. "Well, what do you think?" he asked.

"I don't know."

After remembering the day we'd rode through the rain at Easter and how uncomfortable it had been, I hoped that the answer would be no. I wanted to ride as much as possible, of course, but there were limits.

"We'd be struck by lightning if we went out in this," said Rosie again.

111

Tom laughed, but Mr. Butler said, "It's not a laughing matter, Tom. You could easily be struck, so we won't take any risks. Besides, it's no weather for being outdoors. Stay in here or come back over to the house and watch DVDs until lunchtime. Then we'll see."

He splashed back to the house. Tom, Camilla and Megan grumbled about not riding, but I thought they were being silly. How could anyone want to ride in this? For once, I had a lot more sympathy with Rosie and Emily.

The rain continued to pour down. We all wandered across to the house and lounged about watching DVDs, but the atmosphere was strangely subdued and there were none of the jokes or fooling around of the last few days. I wondered if it was going to be like this till Saturday, which meant things would be a lot less fun. We ate sandwiches for lunch and then gathered on the porch, looking up at the sky. The rain had eased slightly, but it still splashed noisily on the porch roof. I thought about the swallows and whether their nest was soaked. The roof protected the nest, so hopefully they'd be safe and dry.

At last the rain became a series of slow, echoing drops and then finally it stopped. The black clouds had already turned to gray; now they parted and a sliver of sunlight snaked through to light up the tack room so that it glowed.

"Look, there's a rainbow!"

The arc of color linked the farmhouse with the pony paddock. The gap in the clouds widened and the sun started to give out instant heat. There was steam everywhere – from the ground, from the roofs, and, after we'd run down to the paddock, from the ponies, who had gathered under a group of trees as if for warmth and comfort in the storm.

Caroline had been absent all morning but she appeared now and told us to catch ponies and bring them into the yard. Bilbo came willingly enough and seemed to enjoy being rubbed down energetically with a wisp of straw.

"We'll have to wait until evening to do them properly, when the mud's had time to dry," called Caroline.

Great, I thought. Just when we're tired again. Sometimes

grooming ponies made me appreciate what Mom says about housework never ending.

We tacked up and then we went into the paddock again, leading the ponies. We tied them to the fence and then perched next to them while Mr. Butler told us about the next two days.

"There's a horse show in the next village all day on Saturday," he explained, "and you've all been entered. Now it's not a big event, not like some of you'll have been involved in before," – he looked at Camilla and Georgie as if daring them to object, – "but for some of you it'll be your first chance to be in a show. More importantly, it'll be the first chance for most of the ponies, so don't expect too much from them."

I thought back to the pony books I'd read. "Which classes will we be entering?" I asked.

To my relief, no one snickered, so I'd gotten the right terminology.

"You can all show your pony. Then there's a simple jumping competition. If you do well in that you can go on to more advanced jumping. And there'll be gymkhana games."

I knew about those. At Easter we'd finished the week with a day of games – bending, a potato race, a dress-up race and finally a massive treasure hunt, which Mike and I had won. It had been a great day and I was looking forward to having a shot at the same games again. The showing I wasn't sure about. I didn't really know what it involved. And the jumping – well, after yesterday I supposed I could do it a bit, but the idea of jumping in front of a crowd of strangers made me weak at the knees.

"Now, we're going to concentrate on showing this afternoon," Mr. Butler continued. "I know the ponies aren't perfectly groomed because of the storm, but we'll pretend they are. And we'll do some jumping later on, and then a lot more tomorrow. So don't worry if you're not too confident. There's plenty of time to get there."

We mounted and spent the next couple of hours working very hard. First we had to walk the ponies in a big circle, and Caroline and Mr. Butler told each one of us about our faults. I had tons. I wasn't sitting straight enough, my toes were pointing down, and my reins were either too long or too short but never just right. We rode without stirrups for ages, and we had to knot the reins and

113

cross our arms too. It felt precarious – as if I were balanced on a rocking horse. I was far more aware than usual of Bilbo's narrow back, of the swaying motion as he took each pace, and of the way he dropped his head every now and then.

"The idea of this is to stop you from hanging on with the reins," said Caroline, who stood in the middle watching us. "You should use the reins to communicate with your pony, not to stay on board."

Then we had to hold onto the saddle pommel and, still with the stirrups crossed in front of us, go into a sitting trot.

"It's so painful," Phil called after a while. "Can't we do a rising trot?"

"Not without stirrups," said Caroline. "There's nothing to rise against."

I tried and she was right, but I did manage a little rise now and then. But actually, it felt more comfortable to stay down in the saddle, moving with the pony.

"Is there anything I can do to get Rolo to hold his head higher?" asked Tom.

"Well, the main thing is not to do it with the reins," said Mr. Butler, surprisingly. "Of course, you can't now, but you should never haul the pony's head up."

"Except when he's grabbing grass when you're riding," said Rosie.

I remembered how difficult I'd found that when I started with Tim last year. Bilbo wasn't such a greedy pony, but there had still been quite a few times when he'd dropped his head to eat grass and I'd had to get rebalanced and pull his head up.

"Not even then, said Mr. Butler. "If you sit down in the saddle well enough and use your legs right, the pony will work with his hindquarters and that will make his forehand lighter and he'll raise his head."

That sounded like wishful thinking to me.

"Take back your reins and we'll canter," said Mr. Butler.

"Without stirrups?" I said, alarmed.

"Don't worry, it's easy," Megan reassured me from behind. "Just keep your legs long."

I wasn't too sure about that, but when we went into canter (and

I didn't have to do anything as Bilbo just followed the others) I saw what Megan meant. Letting my legs stretch down as far as possible made it far easier to stay securely in the saddle.

"So why do we shorten stirrups to canter when this is easier?" asked Emily when we'd slowed to a walk again.

"Yeah, we'd be like cowboys in the movies. They have really long stirrups and those saddles that stick up in front and behind so you can't fall out," said Phil.

"Why don't we use them, then?" asked Tom. "Wouldn't it be better for trekking?"

"Maybe, but that's a whole different style of riding," Mr. Butler explained. "In Western riding, the bridle's different too. You only hold the reins in one hand, usually the left one."

"But how do you get the pony to turn?" asked Georgie. "I mean, we all ride with one hand holding the reins sometimes, but if you want to take a sharp turn you need both."

"It's complicated, but basically it's a technique called neck reining."

We all tried. I could make Bilbo move to the left, but I couldn't turn him to the right.

"It's a delicate movement," said Phil, who'd been more successful, "but I prefer the usual way."

"These ponies have been trained to respond to classic aids," said Caroline. "They'd have been broken in differently if they'd been going to be ridden Western style."

"It'd be wicked fun to go on a riding vacation in Texas or somewhere," said Camilla dreamily. "You go up into the hills and round up cattle."

"I'm sure you'd pick up the technique easily enough," said Caroline. "It's something I'd love to do too, if I could ever afford it."

Mr. Butler told us to stop the ponies, and then spent a while lecturing us for not stopping them properly. Apparently too many of us were just pulling on the reins and expecting the pony to stop. I felt myself turning red. That's what I always did.

"Remember, you're just giving your pony a signal to stop. You're not actually pulling him to a standstill, as if he had brakes," Mr. Butler explained.

"But how will she know I want her to stop?" asked Rosie, leaning forward to pat Twinkle's neck.

"Your whole body tells her. Sit straighter, push your heels down, squeeze the reins a little tighter and press with your legs."

"But that's what I do to go faster," I said, puzzled.

"Not really. You lean a little bit forward then and you loosen the reins. Let's try. Walk on, everyone."

We tried it and certainly the transition, as it's called; to walk, and then from walk to trot, from trot back to walk, and finally to a halt, felt much smoother and more controlled.

Camilla and Georgie complained they were bored and asked if they could practice reining back.

"It never hurts to go back over the basics," said Caroline, "but yes, have a try. The ponies aren't too used to it, though."

We watched as they concentrated hard and somehow got their ponies to take a few steps backwards. I couldn't see what was happening.

"Tell the others," suggested Mr. Butler.

"You give leg aids, as if you were going forward," explained Camilla, "but you keep the reins really tight."

That didn't seem too hard. We all had a try. Bilbo refused to move in any direction until Caroline came and held his reins right up by his mouth and urged him backwards. He did take a single step back then, but I didn't feel like it had anything to do with me. Twinkle and Star were both doing it beautifully, and Tim and Magpie continued to step back delicately and carefully under the twins. Tom couldn't get Rolo to move either, even when Mr. Butler tried to help.

"Don't bother," he said. "I've done it before, so I know what to do. But Rolo's unhappy with it, so I won't bother."

He gave Rolo a friendly slap on the side. Startled, Rolo stepped back dramatically and we all laughed at Tom's open-mouthed surprise.

Emily was working very hard with Mr. Man, and after a lot of patience she got him to step back nicely. Everyone clapped and she looked pleased and proud.

Phil, on the other hand, hardly tried at all. He said it was it too much like hard work. Mr. Butler looked disapproving but didn't say anything.

After that we had an hour's break and played basketball in the yard while the ponies stood in a long line at the paddock fence. They weren't allowed to go and graze as we were going to ride them again, but I felt sorry for them and sneaked a few mouthfuls of grass to Bilbo and Tim. They looked very funny with the grass hanging out of each side of their munching jaws.

"Not when they're bridled, Jess!" shouted Mr. Butler, seeing me.

"And just leave my pony alone," hissed Georgie, unhitching Tim and taking him further down the line.

Oh no, I'd annoyed her again, and it really hadn't been on purpose. I hadn't even chosen to feed Tim – he'd happened to be next to Bilbo, that's all. I muttered that I was sorry and then we were told to remount and it all got forgotten, except that I had a sneaking feeling that every time I went near Tim, something went wrong.

Chapter Eleven

Caroline showed us how to take off the saddles and wait in a neat line to be inspected by a judge. Mr. Butler pretended to be the judge and asked a lot of difficult questions about how we took care of our ponies. When he asked what I did with mine in the winter I said, "I don't know," and then felt foolish.

"Well, I don't," I said defensively. "I'm not here."

"Lots of people show riding school ponies," said Caroline. "So you're more or less like them."

"What do we say, then?" asked Megan.

"Why not say that the ponies belong to the riding center, but that you know that in the winter they stay outside with rugs on when the weather's cold?" suggested Caroline.

"And we could say about pony nuts," said Rosie eagerly. "They get those as extra food in winter, don't they?"

"Quite right, but they also get a hay net each and every day. They don't need too many pony nuts when they're not working, except when it's really cold."

"Don't they ever come indoors?" I asked, feeling sorry for them.

"They're not used to it, so they wouldn't like it. Captain's stabled, of course, but he's a lot more delicate even though he's so much bigger. Ponies are tough."

"Do you do any riding vacations in winter?" asked Phil.

"It depends on the weather. We mostly do day trips. That way, if it's pouring rain or snowing, we can cancel."

I imagined what it would be like riding along snowy paths and seeing the hills bare and lifeless in winter. I'd seen the area in spring and summer. If only we lived nearer and I could come and ride all year round …

"Right, enough of all this gabbing. A little jumping and we'll call it a day."

We rode down to the bottom of the paddock where a whole series of low poles, supported on crosses of wood, had been set up. Mr. Butler said they were called cavaletti. We had to start at one end and trot through the course, which was fun. Then some people had a try at cantering through, but I'd decided I'd had enough for one day and held back. Tom raced down the course going faster and faster and then flew off Rolo at the last pole. He landed with a thump onto his back, but he jumped up immediately and said he was fine. He'd let go of the reins as he fell and Rolo cantered away. He couldn't catch him for ages, and meanwhile Emily also fell off, more of a slide than an actual fall. Then Bramble stumbled and Phil rolled off sideways.

"You're all getting tired," said Mr. Butler, as Phil got up and shook himself. "Time to stop."

"But I want another turn," said Georgie.

"I think your pony's had enough, even if you haven't."

Tom finally returned leading Rolo, looking hot and sweaty.

"Can I take the jumps once more just to make sure I can do it?" he asked.

"Just the once. We don't want you to lose your nerve."

Georgie looked understandably put out as Tom cantered quickly up to the jumps. Again he went fast, and at the last cavaletti Rolo refused to jump and swerved away. Without a pause, Tom took him round and tried again. Again he swerved.

"That's enough, Tom," called Mr. Butler. "He's telling you he wants to stop."

"But …"

"No buts. Dismount and lead the ponies back up to the yard, everyone, and get the grooming done."

Tom yanked Rolo's head around angrily to point him uphill. Luckily for him, Mr. Butler didn't see. Phil walked Bramble next to me.

"Are you all right?" I asked.

"Not really, but Butler doesn't care. He's far more interested in Tom. He never said I should have another try."

"Maybe he didn't think you wanted to, " I said. "You didn't hurt yourself badly, did you?"

Phil rubbed his leg and winced as if it hurt a lot. "I wouldn't be surprised if I pulled a tendon," he said.

"You wouldn't be walking if you had," I pointed out.

"Oh, great, we all have to wait around for hours when you fall, but when I come off, I'm making a stink."

"I didn't mean that."

"Forget it," he said, but he didn't. He went off sulking and hardly spoke to anyone all evening. I tried to find out if he was really hurt, but I was sure he wasn't. He only limped if he thought someone was looking. Mrs. Butler looked disappointed when he hardly ate any dinner too; he'd been eating like everyone else all week, but now he'd gotten all picky again.

Tom was in a bad mood too. He and Camilla kept whispering crossly to each other. After supper, Georgie said she was going out. The rest of us played a game of Monopoly, but no one was very enthusiastic, and after a while Rosie and Emily said they were going to bed.

Georgie came back in looking pleased with herself, but didn't say where she'd been. Camilla and she went off together and Megan said, "Ready for bed, Jess?"

"In a minute," I said.

I was still worried about Phil and whether I'd misjudged him. So I went over to the chair where he was curled up reading.

"Phil?"

"Yeah?"

"How's your leg?"

"What do you care? You haven't thought about it all evening."

I opened my mouth to retort that I had and then thought it would be a waste of time. "Okay," I said. "Good night."

I didn't feel like talking when I got upstairs. It had been a disappointing day. No riding all morning, lots of arguments, and now this with Phil. I just hoped that things would be better tomorrow.

When I woke up, I couldn't remember what day it was. I counted back through the week. We'd arrived on Sunday, started trekking on Monday, trekked to the lake on Tuesday, and gotten back to the farm on Wednesday. Then yesterday we'd done training, so today must be Friday. Only two more nights. On Saturday, we'd be going to the show, and then on Sunday we had to leave. I wondered how Mom and Dad and the twins were doing. They must have been having fun on the beach while the weather was so hot. I hoped they hadn't had the same storm as us, though. Tim and Holly would have been scared stiff.

That made me think about today's weather, so I hopped out of bed and opened the curtains. There were some clouds, but they were feathery and high; it looked like a good day. I squinted upwards to see the swallows' nest. It looked the same, so the rain hadn't damaged it.

Megan woke up. We both had showers, got dressed – back into our riding clothes this time – and went down to see the ponies before breakfast.

"Star's been rolling," said Megan in disgust. "Look, he's filthy. I'll have to groom him all over again."

Bilbo wasn't much better.

"Let's do them now, before breakfast," I suggested.

"No, because if we do we won't have anything to do while the others are working. All the ponies are the same."

It was true. The ground was muddy after all the rain and the ponies were splattered with patches of grime. We climbed over the paddock fence and wandered among the ponies, talking to them and stroking them. After a while, Rosie and Emily joined us. They were friendly to Megan, but there was a sort of invisible barrier between them and me. It was as if I'd done something horrible, but I knew I hadn't. Even though I got along well with Megan, I still missed Rosie; I'd thought we'd be such good friends forever after Easter, and only a week ago she'd chosen me to come on the trek with her. Surely it couldn't all be because Emily wanted Rosie to herself? I'd tried hard to leave them alone, after all. Of course, Rosie had been behaving in an annoying way – being so melodramatic about things – but a part of me knew that

121

usually I'd have found that funny rather than irritating. Maybe it was me. Maybe I'd somehow changed into a nastier person? But Megan and Camilla seemed to like me, and so did Tom and Phil. Well, actually, Phil was another problem. He'd been so grumpy all day yesterday, acting like I didn't want to be his girlfriend anymore, but before that... And maybe he really had been hurt by that fall and no one had cared.

I was leaning against Bilbo's warm, sweet-smelling flank while I was thinking about all this. He had his head down and was tearing up grass with rapt concentration, taking a step now and again to move to another juicy tuft. I had to jog to keep up. The others were talking a little way away and I could hear the boys now. I'd have to go and join them or they'd think there was something wrong. Well, maybe there was; but what?

I gave Bilbo a loving pat and he deigned to lift his head enough to nuzzle me briefly before returning to his breakfast.

"Jess!" called Megan. "Come on, we're going in for breakfast."

I ran over. Everyone but Georgie was there, leaning or sitting on the paddock fence in the morning sun, with ponies gathered around them. I made a decision as I ran not to worry about things any more. There were two days left, and there was no way I was going to spoil them.

Later, full of eggs and toast, we caught the ponies and groomed them thoroughly. The mud had dried in clumps and came off easily. I spent a long time brushing Bilbo's tail. His mane was short and spiky, but his tail was long and flowing. After I'd brushed it about a million times it shone, black and beautiful. Then we saddled up and gathered in the paddock.

We warmed up by doing some simple circuits at walks and trots. I tried hard to remember all the things we'd been told yesterday about sitting straighter and using legs more. It did seem to be working. I felt more in control, and I noticed that Bilbo was carrying his head a teensy bit higher, though that might just have been that he wasn't tired. We did some fun exercises, too. We had to touch our toes while the ponies walked. You'd think that was easy, but it wasn't. The first time I tried, I leaned to the left and my right leg automatically went backwards, and then I lost the stirrup. My weight shifted and I found myself slipping headfirst toward the ground. Luckily Bilbo stopped dead, and I was able to put both arms out and go into a forward roll. Everyone laughed as I got up.

"Circus tricks, eh, Jess?" said Caroline, coming over to hold Bilbo steady while I remounted.

"What did I do wrong?" I asked. "No one else fell off."

"You let the opposing leg go back, that's all. Your center of gravity moved and you had to fall – very gracefully, I must say. Let's try again."

We all had another try. This time I glued my right leg to the girth and stayed in the saddle. It was easy after that.

Then we walked on and did arm-swinging movements. Bramble took exception to Phil's doing that and skittered away from the circle, almost unseating him. He quickly gathered the reins and brought her back in just behind me.

"Well done," I said. I hadn't spoken to him yet this morning. "How's your leg?"

"My leg?" He sounded surprised and I thought, yes, I was right, he was making a big deal about nothing yesterday. "Oh, it's better today."

Mr. Butler yelled at us to stop talking and do the next exercise. This involved leaning right back with arms folded until your head touched the pony's back. I found that straightforward, but Emily couldn't get all the way back. She wasn't supple enough, and she said it hurt her stomach muscles to pull herself back up.

"Tom, show us how you did that trick the other day," said Camilla.

We all stopped and watched as Tom flung himself sideways and somehow pulled himself under Rolo's tummy and back up the other side.

"I don't get it; how do you hold on?" asked Emily.

"It's just going quickly," Tom explained. "Think of it like a bar in a gym. It's the same movement."

"Sideways, though," said Georgie, considering. "You have to let yourself down sideways."

"Um, but you change direction as you go," said Tom. He demonstrated again. One or two others tried but no one else could do it, and it hurt when you landed on the grass – as I found when I had a try.

"I can vault onto my pony," said Camilla. She slipped off, took a few steps back, then ran forward and vaulted lightly onto Magpie, who snorted in surprise and nearly threw her off the opposite side.

"That's easy," said Tom. "You just have to go for it."

We all tried and it really was easy. The only problem was if the pony moved suddenly when you were in mid-flight.

Mr. Butler told us to give the ponies a break, so we sat around chatting for half an hour and then took them down to the cavaletti for more practice. That was fine. I felt far more confident and even tried taking the jumps at a canter. Although we seemed to be whizzing along alarmingly fast, the actual jumping was easier. The transition between canter and lift was almost unnoticeable, provided I remembered to lean forward. The only trouble I had was remembering to go back upright at the end of the jumps to slow Bilbo down.

Then it was time for lunch. Afterward we helped put up a bigger jumping course. There were three cavaletti like we were used to, then some straw bales, then a single pole balanced on straw bales, then the stream that wandered through the paddock, then a further cavaletti, only this time two crosspieces were placed on top of each other so the jump was twice as high, then the stream again, and finally a line of double-height straw bales. It took ages to get it all in place and looked very impressive, like a real jumping course, when we'd finished.

"Is this the sort of thing we'll have to jump tomorrow?" I asked.

"In terms of height, yes," said Mr. Butler. "The jumps will look more impressive – large boards painted bright colors and so on – but the technique stays the same. And remember, if there's a jump you don't want to take, you can always skip it."

"We wouldn't win then, though, would we?" said Camilla.

"Well, no."

I thought, OK, you can go for everything, but I'll be very glad not to have to jump something too high.

We took turns on the course. Camilla and Georgie took their ponies over with no trouble at all. Rosie had to encourage Twinkle a lot – in fact, she was allowed to tap her with a stick just before each jump – and got around all the jumps. Megan followed and did a neat round except for the two higher jumps, which she skipped.

"I'll try them next time," she panted when she got back to us.

Phil went next. Bramble hesitated at the stream – she never much liked water – but then popped over perfectly. She took the high cavaletti like a bird, cantered fast towards the stream, and skidded to a stop, her head poked forward, her front legs splayed. Her stop was so sudden that Phil didn't have time to react. He flew over Bramble's head, and landed with a massive splash flat on his face in the center of the stream.

It was very shallow and soft, so no one was worried. But I ran over anyway to grab Bramble and help him stand up, to make up for yesterday. He was soaking wet and his face was like thunder, but as he got up he did a sort of double take, clicked out of his anger, then grinned and waved at everyone in mock-heroic fashion. Accompanied by cheers and laughter, he dripped up to the house while I tied Bramble to the fence.

"Come and have another try when you've changed!" called Mr. Butler. Phil nodded and ran off.

Wow, I thought. That's different from yesterday.

Emily went next and trotted steadily around the course, skipping the high cavaletti but clearing the double-height bales. "They look easier somehow," she explained.

"It's because you can't see a gap underneath," said Camilla. "That's why they fill under jumps with flowers and things, isn't it?"

Mr. Butler nodded in agreement as we watched Tom setting off. "Don't go too fast!" he warned.

Tom steadied Rolo and approached each jump really slowly, sometimes even at a walk. Rolo found the bigger jumps hard from that pace and knocked the poles off and spread straw around.

"Too slow," said Mr. Butler as Tom came back.

"That's not fair!" he protested. "Yesterday you said I went too fast, and now I'm too slow!"

"There's such a thing as a happy medium," said Caroline. "Rolo's powerful, but he can't jump from a standing start."

"I can," said Tom.

"You're not a pony."

Tom shrugged and led Rolo over to Camilla. They talked and giggled together conspiratorially while I mounted Bilbo and rode down to the start of the course.

The first jumps looked so familiar that I took them without really thinking. The single pole was no higher, but Bilbo took off a long way before and clipped the pole so that it thumped to the ground behind us. Bilbo reacted by going faster, so we cantered spastically through rather than over the stream. His ears were twitching as he approached the high cavaletti, and I sat as still as I could, just leaning forward a little, and felt thrilled as we jumped it neatly. Again we splashed through the stream, and then as we approached the final jump he swerved past and pounded up to where everyone was waiting. I pulled him to a halt.

"I think Bilbo took charge there," said Mr. Butler, dryly. "But you stayed on, so well done. Next time, bring him back to a trot or even a walk if he gets too excited."

"It's a good idea to ride a tight circle before you start, and even put one in the middle of the course if things are getting out of hand," advised Caroline. I'd noticed that Camilla and Georgie had ridden like that and I'd wondered why. Now I knew.

"If everyone's happy we'll have another try," announced Mr. Butler. "Caroline, would you mind going back to the tack room for a riding crop for Rosie?"

Caroline went off and we were working out the order we'd ride when Phil came back.

"There's an urgent phone call for you," he said to Mr. Butler.

"Oh, brother! All right, I'll be back in a minute."

Mr. Butler strode off toward the farmhouse. Phil joined me.

"I jumped it all," I said. "Well, Bilbo did. And we skipped the last one. And he didn't really jump the stream."

"But you got around?"

"Really fast!"

"Well done. You'll do even better this time."

"And I'm not nervous any more. Isn't it wicked when you go fast? Like flying."

"I did some real flying this time," he said.

126

"Oh, yes, of course. Are you OK?"

"Yeah, I'm fine. Did it look funny?"

"Hilarious." I smiled at the memory. "And you were very brave not to make a stink."

"Thanks." We looked at each other happily. Bilbo and Bramble obviously felt left out and stuck their long noses between us. Bilbo had been snatching grass and dribbled green slime down my front. It was the most non-romantic moment, and yet the most romantic as well...

There was the sound of hoofs. We looked around and saw that Camilla and Tom had cantered down and were chasing each other over the course. The pace was fast and exciting, and I longed to be part of it. Then, after the stream, instead of turning to the double cavaletti jump, Tom, who was the leader, steered Rolo straight towards the paddock fence. Rolo gathered himself up and cleared the rails easily, but Magpie shuffled to a stop, nearly unseating Camilla.

"What's all that about?" asked Phil.

"Tom dared her," said Megan, joining us. "He said she'd be chicken if she didn't do it."

"It's all right for them. They're fantastic riders," I said. "None of the rest of us could possibly do that jump."

"Couldn't I? Just watch."

It was Georgie. I hadn't realized she was so close, and of course, she was as experienced a rider as Camilla. She vaulted onto Tim, kicked into a canter, and pounded down towards the fence.

"Jess! It's far too high for Tim!" Rosie squeaked.

But Tim – lovely brave Tim – wasn't going to be daunted. He tucked his front feet under him as he pushed off from his strong back legs, and cleared the fence with an inch to spare.

There was a collective sigh of relief from all of us who were watching. Camilla circled Magpie to have another try, but Phil saw Mr. Butler and Caroline coming down the hill behind us and shouted out a warning and she stopped. Tom and Georgie cantered away from us to give themselves space for the jump back. Tom went first, and again Rolo cleared the fence easily. Tim, though, wasn't ready. He hesitated as he got nearer, and then turned and

127

cantered alongside the fence instead of attempting it. Georgie took him back for another try.

"Georgie! What on earth are you doing!" shouted Mr. Butler, and at the same instant Caroline yelled, "Watch out for the bull!"

Suddenly, filling the horizon, there was a massive bull, striding ponderously towards Georgie and Tim. We watchers clutched each other as it accelerated, head down, furious that a rider and pony were on its territory. Tim and Georgie were ahead, galloping now towards the fence, but the bull was getting closer with every stride. Georgie was leaning forward over Tim's neck, urging him on, giving quick glances back at the danger behind her. Tim's eyes were staring and his legs were going so fast they were just a blur. They were approaching the fence, and they'd reached the point where they'd have to take off. If Tim swerved this time or missed, or if Georgie fell off, they could be in truly serious trouble …

Chapter Twelve

I'd never believed the expression about your heart being in your mouth, but it's true. I felt as if I was choking as I stood there, transfixed, waiting for disaster. I didn't even feel Megan's finger-nails digging into my shoulder, though the marks stayed for days afterward. All our attention was on the three figures and the double horizontal poles that should be separating them and weren't.

Even with my limited knowledge of jumping, I could see that Tim was too close. He had to push off almost vertically to get clear. The power in his hindquarters must have been amazing, perhaps fueled by fear. His front legs tucked and then pushed forward, taking his body up and over, and his hind legs lifted just enough – only just, a quarter-inch, perhaps – to scrape over the top pole. Georgie clung precariously on, stirrups flying loose, her body twisted to one side as Tim flew over, so that even at the last possible moment it looked as if she'd fall. And behind, the bull slowed, heavy feet thumping on the ground, small eyes glaring at its lost enemy.

And then they were safely over and Georgie was sliding off, crying, and Tim was standing still, sweating, his sides heaving. Within seconds, they were surrounded. Caroline was checking Tim over and leading him away to calm him down. Camilla was hugging her sister and the rest of us were crowded around, talking noisily, speculating on what might have happened, excited. Mr.

129

Butler spoke to Georgie gently at first, making sure she wasn't hurt. Then, predictably, he was angry.

"What possessed you to jump the fence in the first place? Apart from everything else, you could have lamed Tim for life!"

"I dared Camilla," said Tom, bravely. "So I suppose it's my fault."

Mr. Butler turned on him. "Yes, and it's about time you stopped being so stupid. First the quarry and now this."

"We didn't know there was a bull in there," put in Camilla.

"There's never been anything but sheep there before," said Phil.

"You never told us," said Rosie.

"How was I to know you'd get such a ridiculous idea in your heads?" said Mr. Butler, exasperated.

"Sorry," said Camilla and Tom together.

Caroline came over and said, "Tim's fine, just a bit excited. No damage done."

Mr. Butler turned on Georgie. "So what were you doing? Tim's a lot smaller than Rolo and Magpie. Didn't it occur to you that he might find it too hard?"

Georgie nodded and sniffed.

"I'm sorry too," she said.

Mr. Butler looked around at us all.

"I don't know what to say. Perhaps I should forbid you all to take part in the show tomorrow as a punishment."

"Oh, no!"

"Please don't!"

"It wasn't our fault." That was Emily.

Mr. Butler and Caroline went off in a little huddle to talk. The rest of us stood around looking miserable. Tom said, "What got into you, Georgie? What were you thinking? I never dared you; Tim's too small."

But before Georgie could answer, Mr. Butler came back.

"We've decided to carry on as normal," he said. "We think you've probably learned a useful lesson, and that you were being silly rather than deliberately idiotic. And it is true I didn't mention that my neighbor's put his bull in the field, and the reason I didn't was because I didn't know myself. That's what the phone call was – he was calling to warn me."

There was a babble of talk as we thanked him and Caroline, talked to each other about how we'd felt, debated whether Tim would be OK for tomorrow, and wondered what we'd be doing next, all at the same time. After a while, Mr. Butler shushed us. He looked at his watch.

"It's five o'clock," he said, "and I'd planned a few more rounds of this course today. Are you up for it?"

Everyone was, although Georgie looked nervous as she got back on Tim. Mr. Butler talked to her quietly and then she started to circle Tim at a slow trot, around and around, while the rest of us lined up to jump.

After all the excitement, the course seemed tame. I trotted Bilbo around, and we did it all except for the very last jump. The second time I went faster. I had a moment of fright after the stream when I wondered if Bilbo would suddenly take it into his head to copy the others and jump the fence. Would I be strong enough to stop him? But he didn't even look at the fence; his attention was all on the jumping course. His ears were pricked and alert, and we cantered over the high cavaletti, cleared the stream with a long, stretchy jump, and finally lifted over the double straw bales with no problem at all.

"Great stuff," said Caroline, as I trotted back to the group, but the others were oddly cool, even Megan and Phil, and I had the feeling they'd been discussing me while I was gone.

Georgie had been alternating trotting and walking in a circle all this time, joined at times by Camilla, and now Mr. Butler told her to try the course. She looked worried, so Caroline went down to the far fence to stand there and make sure Tim didn't try to jump it. Not that he would have, I'm sure. He was far too sensible. But I could understand how Georgie would feel.

Georgie got around; not very well, but she looked more confident afterwards. That was the end of the day's riding. We led the ponies back to the yard, dumped the tack and rubbed them down. I was feeling a funny mixture of tiredness, happiness about jumping, worry about the show tomorrow, and a permanent nagging concern about why I seemed to be unpopular. I didn't work as hard as usual over Bilbo's coat. After I'd led him back to the paddock and let

132

him loose I remembered I hadn't checked his feet. Never mind, I thought. There's never anything there, and we've been on grass all day. I'm too tired to get him back.

By the time I got indoors the dinner bell was ringing. I sat between Phil and Camilla at the end of the table and concentrated on eating. Phil was sweet. He said he could see I was tired and that I shouldn't try to talk. Most of Camilla's attention was devoted to Tom. The others all talked and ate noisily. Afterwards, while they were arguing cheerfully about whether to play a game or watch television, or both, I told Megan I had a headache and was going to bed. Mrs. Butler came upstairs after me to check that I was OK. She went on about the fall I'd had the first day; I'd almost forgotten that. I reassured her that all I needed was sleep and got into bed quickly. But I couldn't sleep for ages. My thoughts drifted between the joys of riding and the puzzles of friendships. When Megan crept in, expecting me to be asleep, I lay as quietly as I could. I suppose I must have dropped off in the end, because suddenly it was daylight and the final day of the vacation had started.

My head had cleared, and I felt fresh and energetic. Megan was still asleep so I tiptoed out with my clothes and had a long shower. Then I went downstairs and let myself out, just like Rosie and I had done one morning at Easter. I jogged down to the paddock and sat on the rail. The ponies were scattered all over, some grazing and some just standing. I wondered if they were asleep or thinking – and if ponies do think, and if so, what about. After a while, Bilbo lifted his head from the grass and saw me, and started over. That made me very happy – until I realized that he was limping heavily. Oh no! What had I done?

It was his front foreleg, the one on the left, that was giving him trouble. As he got near, I steadied him by holding his halter rope and ran my other hand down the leg as you do, so that when I reached the hoof he willingly lifted it. I supported its weight on my knee and looked for the problem. There was a gleam of white between the brown of the hoof and the dull iron of the shoe – a stone must have lodged there, and I hadn't bothered to remove it. I couldn't get it out with my fingers, so I tied Bilbo to the fence and ran to get a hoof

133

pick from the tack room. There was a sick feeling in my stomach. Rosie could have prophesied doom as much as she liked and I'd have believed her.

Phil and Tom were just coming out of the cottage and joined me. They watched as I extracted a large, sharp flint and Tom whistled in dismay.

"I know, I know," I said unhappily. "I've lamed him."

"You didn't, Jess, it was the stone that did that," said Phil, putting a comforting arm round my shoulders. "It's not your fault."

"But I didn't check!" I wailed.

"Let him walk and we'll see," suggested Tom.

I unhitched the rope and led Bilbo while they watched.

"It's no good, is it?" I said. "He's still lame."

They nodded.

"We'd better tell Butler," said Tom. "Shall I…?"

He disappeared and Phil and I leaned against each other miserably.

"I was so looking forward to the show," I said. "Bilbo and I have been getting along so well."

Phil stroked my arm and said nothing.

"So what's all this?" boomed Mr. Butler's cheerful early morning voice. He patted Bilbo, examined his hoof expertly, walked him for a few paces, and said, "Well, I'm afraid you're right. He won't be fit to be ridden for a day or two. The frog's badly bruised."

I didn't like to ask what he was talking about at the time, but later I checked in a pony book and discovered that the frog is the soft tissue under the foot.

"Don't look so upset, Jess," he went on. "These things happen."

"I forgot to check his feet last night," I said in a small voice.

"Well, you won't forget again, will you? He could've picked it up during the night, anyway. There are some stones like that in the stream and every now and then they give problems."

I felt less guilty, but the ponyless day still loomed ahead.

"Can Jess share Bramble?" said Phil suddenly.

I clutched his hand in gratitude and he squeezed mine back.

"No need," said Mr. Butler cheerfully. "Have you forgotten the other ponies?"

134

"But you said they needed to rest this week."

"True, and they've had a rest. We'll sort something out, don't you worry. Come up to the house for breakfast, and I'll tell you what'll happen after that."

I gave Bilbo a guilty hug and watched him limp down towards the long grass near the stream. Poor Bilbo. I'd distrusted him so much at first, and he'd turned out to be so sweet and hadn't even nipped me for two days. I felt as though I deserved to be nipped now.

"Come on," urged Phil. "I'm hungry."

That took my mind off Bilbo. "Wow, you're hungry? For the food here?"

"For the food here. Do you know, when we got back from the trek, I didn't eat much and I felt grumpy and tired."

"I noticed."

"So I thought about it, and wondered if the two things were connected. I can't exactly say I love the food here, but I do feel better after eating it."

Sure enough, he ate as much sausage and fried eggs as anyone else that morning. I pushed away my feelings about Bilbo and ate too. Hadn't Mr. Butler promised me another pony? Maybe it'd be Meg, the lovely, delicate light roan that Jane had ridden at Easter.

Everyone was busily discussing the show, so I didn't mention what had happened. In fact, I didn't say anything. Somehow a wall of dislike had built up between me and Rosie, Emily and Georgie. Plus the others kept looking at me awkwardly as if I were embarrassing them. Afterwards, we gathered in the common room. Mr. Butler came in with a sheaf of papers.

"In a minute, I want you all to go upstairs and get yourselves dressed tidily for the show. If you've brought other riding clothes, this is your chance to wear them. Neat tied-back hair, girls, please, and polished boots, everyone. Then you do a thorough grooming session, and we'll set off at eleven to ride to the show. It's only half an hour away. My wife is bringing the car with lunch and drinks, so you don't have to worry about that." He looked around at all our excited faces. 'Now, these are the entry forms for the show today, so take one each and put your name and address, plus the name of the center. Then write in your pony's name and me as the owner. OK?"

He started handing them out and then stopped. "Oh, I forgot to say. Bilbo's gone lame, unfortunately. So I'm swapping Jessica onto Tim for today and Georgie can ride Campbell. You'll be fine on him, Georgie, but he's too strong for Jess."

There was a moment of absolute silence.

Then Georgie gave me the blackest of black looks and ran from the room.

Later on, while we saddled up, Camilla brought Magpie over to Tim and me.

"Don't worry about Georgie," she said. "She's being weird, but that happens sometimes."

"I feel terrible about her losing Tim!" The words burst out of me and I wanted to cry but held back the tears by screwing up my eyes and clenching my fists.

"I don't really know what's gotten into her. She won't talk to me."

"That must be hard when you're identical twins," I said.

"Umm, she's been talking to the other girls, but not to me. I get kind of jealous, you know, but then I don't necessarily tell her everything I think either. I used to. Just not now that we're growing up."

I thought once more of my twins and how complicated life can be.

"Never mind," I said awkwardly. "She'll get over it, whatever it is. I just wish Bilbo hadn't gone lame."

"Sure you do," said Rosie in a hard voice, leading Twinkle by and giving me a look that felt like a dagger. "You got what you wanted all along."

"What are you talking about?"

"Don't fake, Jess. We all knew how sad you were when Georgie got Tim. Well, now all your scheming's paid off. You've got him back."

"Funny about the bull, wasn't it?" said Emily, scathingly, dogging Rosie's footsteps as usual.

I stood open-mouthed as they marched off. Was this what was behind all the coldness? But why? Yes, I'd been upset when I

136

couldn't have Tim, but I'd gotten over that fast enough. I'd loved having Bilbo for the last couple of days. And what did Emily mean about the bull?

I turned to Camilla but she had her back to me. She was pulling at Magpie's girth as if it was difficult to fasten. I didn't think it was. She didn't want to look at me. I put an urgent hand on her shoulder.

"Camilla, I need to talk. What's going on?"

She didn't look round. "I don't know. I thought ... I don't know."

She wouldn't say anything more. No one would. Even Phil and Megan looked embarrassed and kept away from me. Miserably, I finished tacking Tim up and led him out to the center of the yard to be checked by Mr. Butler. He did a thorough inspection, including a pointedly close look at Tim's feet, and then said, "Fine. Pleased to have Tim back, Jess?"

I nodded dumbly. No way did I want to get him involved in all this. That would make me even more unpopular.

Meanwhile, most of the others had mounted and the last ones were being inspected hurriedly. No one came near me. I stroked Tim's neck awkwardly. I hadn't had a chance to feel pleased to have him again. It had all been spoiled by what had happened, and although in a way it felt lovely to be riding him again, and to stroke his soft gray neck and feel his beautiful pale mane cascade over my hands, none of it was worthwhile. Across the yard, Georgie was ready on Campbell. Caroline had gone after her when she'd left the common room, and when they'd reappeared all the others had been really nice to her, especially Rosie. Megan and Phil huddled their ponies together, whispering to each other and avoiding looking at me.

The ride to the show should have been such fun. We walked and trotted the ponies along familiar lanes to the village where we'd bought souvenirs last Easter. The show was in a field just past it. Everywhere there were ponies and horses and excited riders and horse trailers and all the trappings of a show. It was just like I'd read about and imagined so many times. Here I was, in what should have been a perfect situation, having a horrible time.

The trouble was, there was no time to talk to anyone and work things out. We'd left late, so the moment we arrived at the field, we had to be ready for the showing class. We had a quick check that the ponies still looked good, and then we joined another ten or so riders and ponies in the big ring. I didn't even have a chance to look around to see if Mom and Dad and the twins were among the families that were scattered on the grass. There were no big stands of seats or anything like that – just a few posts stuck in the ground with a rope connecting them to make a big ring, where we were, and a smaller one, where some little children on tiny ponies were playing some sort of game. Even that short glance around meant I'd lost concentration. Tim had been following the others walking around, and I realized that I wasn't sitting straight or applying aids or anything. I was being carried along like a complete beginner. Blushing, I pulled myself together, sitting upright with my legs tight to Tim's sides, tightening the reins to be ready for the command to trot.

Although we'd trotted on the way, I still wasn't completely used to Tim after Bilbo, and I didn't start posting immediately. The judge was an outdoorsy woman who stood in the center and smiled encouragingly at everyone, but I was sure she'd seen and dismissed me as no good. Sure enough, when she called people into the center to ride figures of eight, I wasn't among them. Megan was, and Tom and Camilla, and two strangers.

Then we all had to stand in a line and dismount and take off the saddles. Tim looked beautiful and the judge gave me an approving nod, though I didn't feel even that was entirely justified. After all, it had been Georgie who'd been looking after Tim all week, not me.

The first three were called forward and presented with rosettes. Tom came third, a strange girl second, and Camilla, who looked amazing in a black jacket, cream jodhpurs and gleaming boots, riding an equally gleaming Magpie, was awarded the first place.

We crowded around to exchange high fives and congratulate them. Even though the rest of us hadn't done so well, there was a sort of reflected glory on all of us trekkers. For a moment, everyone seemed to forget that they hated me. But then they remembered and I was shunned again.

138

Phil came over to me, though, as we led the ponies over to the gymkhana ring. The tinies were finishing a game of musical statues. Their ponies were so sweet; a couple of Shetlands with short legs and barrel tummies, and an assortment of other eager, sturdy ponies.

Phil said, looking at the ponies rather than at me, "Did you really do all those things, Jess?"

"What things?" I said defensively.

"Emily and Rosie say ..."

"It would be them," I said angrily. "Emily's spent the whole week trying to make Rosie hate me. Well, she seems to have succeeded, doesn't she?"

"But what they're saying..."

I grabbed Phil's arm. "Come over here where we can talk and you tell me exactly what they're saying. How can I defend myself against a pack of lies when I don't even know what they are?"

Phil allowed me to drag him away from the ring. Tim and Bramble followed obediently.

"Well?" I said.

Phil wouldn't meet my eyes.

"I wouldn't have believed them if there hadn't been so many things going on," he muttered. "I didn't for most of the week."

"Believe what?" I was shouting now. People were looking at us. Mr. Butler hurried over and told us to join the others for the bending race.

"In a minute," I said. "Please, just give us a minute."

Mr. Butler looked puzzled, but someone called him and he went back to the others.

"Tell me," I said in a calmer voice. "What have I done that's so awful?"

"Well, we all knew you were upset about not getting Tim," he started, sounding really embarrassed.

"Yes, but I didn't go on about it. I got used to Bilbo."

"You fell off him."

"I didn't blame Bilbo. Well, not much."

"Georgie apparently got fed up with you always feeding Tim and stuff."

"And that makes me some kind of evil person?"

"No, no. But there was the girth that came loose, and then her saddlebag fell off in the lake."

"So? What did that have to do with me?"

"Well, according to Rosie, you'd been near Tim just before both times."

I considered. "I might have been. But I didn't touch her girth or her bag. That would be wrong. What else?"

"Emily says you were mean to Georgie by the quarry."

"When she said I hit her?"

Phil nodded.

"But I didn't! She just yelled for no reason! Or she got stung. I don't know." I felt helpless. "Why would I want to hurt her, anyway?"

"She hurt her knee in the first place when you said you'd catch her."

"Phil! She put all her weight on my bad shoulder! I just couldn't take it."

Phil shrugged.

"Is that it?" I asked.

"You did make her fall into that pile of poop," he said. "We all saw that."

"I didn't! That farmer slapped Bilbo and he rushed into Tim. And I said sorry."

"You laughed."

"We all laughed. Anyway, if all this was against me, how come you and Camilla and Megan were still my friends?"

"We all thought Rosie and Emily and Georgie were being stupid. Well, actually, Georgie didn't say anything about it all, but the other two, you know …"

"So what changed things?"

"The bull."

"The bull!"

"Rosie said –"

"You were there, Phil! Remember! It was only yesterday. I said something about Camilla and Tom being the only riders good enough to jump the fence. I never even looked at Georgie."

Phil went quiet. "You're right," he said after a bit. "That's all you said. I suppose it was on top of everything else."

"But there wasn't anything else!"

Yes, but Rosie and Emily say you must have seen the bull earlier, before breakfast, when you were on your own at the bottom of the paddock."

"I didn't! Can't you believe me? Why would I suddenly turn into such a disgusting person? Why would I put everyone into danger – and the ponies too?"

"You really and truly didn't do any of the other things?"

"I stroked Tim and gave him some grass every now and again. That's all."

There was a silence, broken by a ragged cheer from behind us. I'd forgotten all about the gymkhana.

"Camilla didn't think I was evil," I said. "Well, at least not until today."

"That's true. Megan, too."

"So it's my word against Emily's and Rosie's. Has anyone even bothered to ask Georgie?"

"She said you lamed Bilbo so that you'd get Tim for today."

"Oh, great!"

"I don't think you did. Tom and I saw how upset you were this morning. You're right. Georgie hasn't exactly confirmed anything else. It just all sort of built up."

"And you'd all trust her rather than me."

"Well, no," said Phil unhappily. "I'm beginning to think it's all been a mistake. I can understand how you must have felt about Tim. I'd hate to come here and not get Bramble. But it wouldn't be like you to behave like we've been thinking." He swallowed hard. "I'm sorry, Jess."

I felt as if a bubble of tension had burst. I smiled at him gratefully. He leaned forward and gave me the tiniest of kisses on the lips.

"Come on, you two. What are you up to?" called Caroline.

"I'll tell the others," offered Phil.

"No. Tell Camilla and Megan, and maybe Tom. Let them tell the others," I said. "I need them to believe in me first, or the other three won't."

141

"OK."

We pulled up the ponies' heads. They'd been grazing surreptitiously and looked comical and messy with green shoots sticking out from their chomping jaws. We scrambled up and gathered reins before trotting over to the ring. I felt so much better now that everything was out in the open. Before long, hopefully, my friends would be my friends again.

But I couldn't help wondering what Georgie was up to.

Chapter Thirteen

The rest gave us curious sideways looks when we joined them We were bustled straight into a potato race. I knew about that one. You have to ride as fast as you can to a sack of potatoes, collect one at a time, and get as many as possible into a bucket at the other end of the course. They'd set the sacks of potatoes up high so we didn't have to dismount. That meant the ponies could go really fast. There were several heats, but I was in the first one, with several people I didn't know and Megan. We went to opposite ends of the line, and once the whistle blew I didn't have time to think about her. I'd done well in this race at Easter, and there was a sudden feeling of familiarity as I kicked Tim into a fast canter for the first potato. He must've loved the game as much as I did. I hardly had to do anything to control him. He tore up and down the course and whizzed around at each end. The only problem was me getting the potatoes into the bucket. When the whistle blew again, I became aware of the others for the first time and looked in their buckets. Mine looked fullest – and it was. We were through to the finals!

I patted Tim enthusiastically to thank him and led him over to the shade of a tree on our own to watch the others. Emily and Georgie were in the next heat. I could see Phil talking earnestly to Megan and Camilla. Megan was having trouble keeping Star still after the race. Then Phil and Camilla were called for the next heat, together with Rosie, and Megan slipped off Star and led him over to me.

"Phil's been telling us," she said. "I didn't think you'd been horrible, it was only this morning …"

"I know," I broke in, "It must have looked very suspicious on top of everything else. Except there was no everything else."

"I know." She hugged me and I felt so much happier. If she and Phil believed me, I didn't care so much about the others.

Phil cantered over excitedly. "I'm in the finals with you, Jess," he said.

"Well done! We weren't watching..."

"Never mind. Let's see if Tom gets through."

The three of us left the ponies tethered to a long, low branch and squashed up together to watch the fourth heat. Tom and Rolo powered through the race, winning easily. I didn't think there'd be much competition for him in the finals after that, but I was wrong. The final was between Tom, Phil, me, and a local boy on a tall skinny pony that flashed around incredibly fast and beat us all soundly. Tom came in second, and Phil and I tied for third, so we were all happy. I got a real rosette to pin on Tim's brow band.

Tom had never really gotten involved in all the hubbub about me, but after the race I saw Camilla take him to one side, and then they both treated me like normal. I felt awkward with Camilla. After all, it was her sister who was the center of everything. But there was no time for more talk – we'd all been entered in the sack race and the next half-hour was a happy scramble of jumping on and off ponies, wrestling our way into ancient, holey sacks, and trying to lead the excited ponies while sack-hopping. I lost my heat, but Rosie and Phil got through to the finals. Phil got a second place.

"Not bad," I said, looking at the two rosettes on Bramble's noseband.

"It's the jumping this afternoon that I want to do well in," he said. "Games are fun, but jumping shows how well you can ride."

"Not much hope for me, then," I said, "but who cares? This is fun."

We had a break for lunch. Mrs. Butler had laid out a spectacular picnic under the trees, and the ponies were tied up in the shade and given water and some hay to nibble. Rosie and Emily were still not talking to me, but they were clearly puzzled that everyone else was. Except Georgie, and, as usual, she ate quickly and disappeared.

"Where does she go?" I asked Camilla quietly, bolder now that we'd worked things out.

"Don't tell anyone, but she's got a phone," she said.

"A phone! But I saw her hand hers in on Sunday."

"She's got two."

I thought back to when Mr. Butler collected the phones and remembered that Georgie had seemed oddly pleased with herself.

"Is there someone special she's phoning?" I asked.

Camilla sighed. "I don't know. She's being really secretive. That's partly what I was talking about earlier."

"Has she got a boyfriend?"

"Georgie? No!" She sounded surprised at the very idea. The beginnings of a theory began to form in my mind.

"Jess!"

It was Mom, carrying Tim (my brother, not the pony!). I rushed over to hug both of them.

"Where's Dad?"

"He's coming with Holly. They're looking at the ponies."

"They can't just look at any ponies, you've got to look at ours," I said firmly. I ran over to Dad who was bumping the stroller along the ground. Holly was inside, bouncing up and down with delight.

Everyone crowded around to meet the twins, even the boys, who went all gaga over them. I introduced my Mom and Dad to Mr. and Mrs. Butler and to Caroline.

"Which one's Rosie?" Dad asked, looking around.

Slightly reluctantly, Rosie came forward and shook hands. I introduced Phil, Megan and Camilla, and then Mom and Dad settled down on the rugs with the twins. We all went to get ready for the jumping.

I felt proud of Tim as I sat on him at the entrance to the big ring. His gray coat shone and he looked alert and intelligent. He stood very still, except for an occasional shake of his head. I could see he was watching the jumping carefully, ready for his turn.

There were twenty or so entries for the novice jumping. Camilla had looked rather snooty at the idea of being a novice, but Mr.

146

Butler had emphasized that it was the ponies that were novices rather than us. I was just relieved that I wasn't being asked to do too much. The course was terrifying when seen from the ground. From on top of Tim, it looked more manageable. Caroline told us that the fences were no higher than we'd been jumping, but they looked higher because they were properly built.

I was the fourth to jump, and I have to say I didn't cover myself in glory. In fact, I only cleared two of the jumps. Tim's hoofs toppled four others, either as he took off or as he went over, and he refused another three times, so we were disqualified. I walked him back feeling very silly, but much to my surprise Mom and Dad were thrilled.

"You were fantastic," said Dad. "I had no idea you could do all that."

"I can do those sort of jumps normally," I tried to explain. "It's only here."

"We couldn't be prouder if you'd won," said Mom, stroking Tim. "You've only ridden for a few days, and look at you."

"We'll have to see if we can manage a few lessons back home," suggested Dad.

"Or maybe I could come back here soon?" I pleaded.

"We'll talk about it. Look, isn't that Rosie jumping now?"

Rosie did better than I had; she got around the whole course and only knocked down two jumps. The loudspeaker announced eight faults.

Camilla rode a beautiful clear round soon after, and Tom scraped by with one too, despite tapping practically every fence on the way.

"He must've stuck them on with glue," giggled Megan, next to me.

A while later, it was Phil's round. He looked very tense and was holding Bramble on a very tight rein. She bucked a couple of times as they circled, and then they crossed the starting line and set off at a rapid pace. They cleared the jumps faster and faster, skimming them but never quite touching, until the very end. Bramble approached at a gallop, took off too early, and demolished the fence with her front legs. Phil clung on and brought her back to a canter and then a trot.

"Well done!" we chorused.

147

"Yeah, well, it wasn't me so much as Bramble. She got the bit between her teeth that time!"

"A little steadier another time?" murmured Mr. Butler, and Phil grinned back.

No one else from the trek distinguished themselves, but it was fun watching everyone. One girl shouted "Hup!" before every jump and made us all giggle. Another used a riding crop so hard that I'm pleased to say she was disqualified. Most people got around with four or eight faults, and the odd refusal. I was among the worst, but then, I'd hardly started jumping. I'd do better next time. Now that almost everyone was being friendly again, I was happy and excited, and I really didn't care if I did well or not.

Georgie was almost the last to jump. She circled Campbell several times and then went for the first jump. Campbell cantered up to it, and stopped dead. Georgie nearly went over his head, but recovered well and took him back in another circle. Again, he refused. Mr. Butler ducked under the rope and took her a crop, but even though she gave Campbell a good thwack he still refused, and the loudspeaker crackled, "Disqualified."

She looked so disappointed. I had a sudden brainwave.

"Is it too late for her to ride Tim?" I asked Mr. Butler.

He looked at the two riders waiting to go.

"Probably not. That's a nice thought, Jess."

He grabbed Campbell's reins and spoke to Georgie as she rode out disconsolately. She brightened immediately. He went over to tell the show people, and I slipped off Tim and took Campbell.

Camilla steadied Tim as Georgie mounted.

"This is Jess's idea," she said quietly.

"Is it? Oh. Well, thanks," she said, rather grudgingly.

She took him back to the waiting area, and a few minutes later she was entering the ring again. Tim looked energetic and collected, trotting neatly and then extending into a lovely smooth canter. Even though he wasn't "my" pony any more, I felt a thrill of pride as he cleared each jump. Unfortunately, though, at the fence before last, a wall of alarming-looking bricks – though I knew from experience that they were actually very light – Tim stumbled, and Georgie had a fall. She picked herself up and scrambled back

148

on, took Tim back and cleared the wall, and then just clipped the final fence so that the top pole bounced to the ground.

"I've damaged my knee again," she wailed as she joined us. "A muscle's torn. It's agony!"

Mrs. Butler and my mother helped her off and she lay on the rugs, moaning with pain. Camilla knelt beside her solicitously, and had to be called away by Caroline to ride in the jump-off between her, Tom and two other riders.

"I can't leave her," she said, in tears herself.

"Don't worry. The doctor's on his way," Mrs. Butler said. "We'll keep an eye on her."

Camilla obviously hated leaving her sister, but everyone said she had to, even Georgie who whispered through clenched teeth that Camilla should go.

Reluctantly, Camilla nodded and mounted Magpie. We all patted him and wished her luck. She trotted Magpie into the ring and cantered slowly towards the first jump. Magpie cleared it neatly, and accelerated toward the next. He was obviously excited and wanted to go too fast, but Camilla was a strong enough rider to hold him in. I could just about see that she was placing him exactly before each jump, so that he'd take off at the right moment – all that stuff about strides that I still had to learn. I could see what a skilled rider Camilla really was during that round. She actually rode her pony, whereas half the time I was only being a passenger, and she seemed to be able to predict all the potential hazards and allow for them. It was no surprise when she cantered back to the start with "Clear round" echoing from the loudspeakers. It was almost drowned out by our cheers.

The two unknown competitors each knocked down a fence. Tom was the last to go. This time he decided to let Rolo have his head, like he'd done in the paddock. He galloped around the course, rattling fences and knocking down poles with cheerful abandon. He rejoined us, grinning broadly.

"That was amazing," he said. "After we knocked down the first fence, I thought we'd just have fun, and we did. It was like being on a racehorse!"

So Camilla was the winner – another rosette and a small silver cup.

149

"You'll have to come back next year to compete for it again," said Caroline, slapping her on the back as she jumped down.

"Magpie's brilliant," she said, hugging him and kissing his nose. "I couldn't ask for a nicer pony."

Then we all remembered Georgie and ran to see how she was. The doctor – the same one who'd seen me on Monday – was examining her, pressing her leg and watching for her reactions. He looked puzzled.

He stood up and took Mr. Butler a few paces away to speak to him quietly. Mr. Butler nodded. He walked over to where the ponies were tethered in a long line and stood by Tim. Then he shouted suddenly, "Oh my God, look at Tim!"

The panic in his voice made us all rush over to see what had happened. Nothing seemed to be wrong. Then we all became aware that Georgie was among us, apparently able to run without difficulty.

"Better now?" asked the doctor, dryly. "I don't think you'll have any more trouble with that leg."

He went back to the first aid tent. The rest of us stood around, puzzled.

"Georgie?" said Camilla hesitantly.

Georgie burst into tears and flung herself into her twin's arms.

Mrs. Butler told the rest of us to get back to our ponies, so that's what we did. Most of us went back to the gymkhana field, but Tom decided he'd try the next jumping competition. Phil looked tempted, but when I said I was going to enter the flag race, he said he would too.

We had a great time. Mom and Dad and the twins were ringside cheering us on as we raced to collect as many flags as we could in the time allowed before pushing them into the holders at the far end of the ring. None of us won, but it was tons of fun. Then there was a balloon race, when we had to burst balloons that were tied to posts. Tim wasn't at all sure he liked the bang as they burst, so we only did one round. The rest of the time Tim sort of danced around nearby and wouldn't take any notice of me. Eventually Caroline called me over and said I should stop trying. Megan won that, though. Star was great and seemed to understand exactly what she should do.

Then there was a break for afternoon snack, so we went back to the picnic area. Tom was looking pleased with himself. He'd done a clear round and would be in the jump-off after the break. We all promised to watch.

"Where are the girls?" I asked Caroline, quietly.

"I don't know – oh look, here they are," said Caroline, through a mouthful of chocolate cake.

Camilla and Georgie had their arms around each other's waists as they came towards us. It was odd to see them like that, so nearly identical and yet not really alike. Camilla looked so much calmer and more confident. Georgie somehow always looked messier and vaguely discontented. They called all of us riders over. Mr. Butler looked surprised, but Caroline murmured something to him and they sat back down with the others.

"How's your leg?" asked Tom. Megan shushed him and he looked surprised. Boys can be so clueless.

"Georgie and I have had a talk," started Camilla, looking around at all of us. "We've agreed for me to explain to you all that none of the things that happened to her this week were anyone else's fault. She ... well, she sort of wanted everyone to notice..."

"I know you'll all think I'm kind of pathetic," said Georgie, hesitantly, "but I kind of enjoyed it when things went wrong."

"So the saddlebag and the girth and everything were you?" said Megan, incredulously.

"All me. I'm sorry."

"You really did fall out of the tree," said Rosie, almost accusingly. "The others saw it happen. They saw Jess not catch you."

I opened my mouth to defend myself, but Megan caught my arm and I stayed quiet.

"That was real," Georgie said, "but Jess couldn't hold me because she'd hurt her shoulder, remember? And my knee wasn't so bad as all that. I – well, I liked it when everyone paid attention to me."

"It wasn't your fault when you fell in horse muck," said Emily, as if she desperately wanted it not to be.

"Not exactly my fault, but no one else's."

"But it was Jess who…"

151

"No. It wasn't Jess," said Camilla firmly. "We established that earlier. Jess didn't do anything."

"But the bull, that was definitely Jess." Emily shot me a venomous look.

"Jess didn't say anything to make me go and jump. I just wanted to prove I could do better than Camilla. The bull, well, that was just bad luck."

"Jess knew the bull was there. She saw it before breakfast," said Emily, flatly, as if it was an absolute fact.

"What are you talking about?" said Tom. "The bull wasn't there at breakfast. Mr. Butler told me it had been put there while we were having lunch."

Emily turned very red. I could feel Rosie looking intently at me but I fixed my gaze entirely on the toes of my boots while this tangled mess was worked out.

"I feel really bad about Jess," said Georgie. "I didn't mean for her to take the blame, but it somehow happened that way. Because of my having Tim, I suppose."

"Not just because of that," said Phil, in a tight voice.

"I don't get it," said Tom. "You let all of us think Jess was a witch just to get yourself some attention?"

"I never said it was Jess."

"You never said it wasn't. You knew exactly what Emily and Rosie were saying about her. You're evil."

I looked up. They were all staring at me. I could feel Megan and Phil on either side of me, their arms resting on mine reassuringly.

"I'm so, so sorry, Jess," whispered Georgie. She looked really pathetic. A wail that I instinctively recognized as Holly's wafted over, and I thought again of all the complications of being a twin. I felt sorry for her, condemned to be always in her sister's shadow, that little bit less pretty, less assured, less talented.

"Just clear up two things," I said. "Who were you phoning, and why did you really scream at the quarry? Was it a wasp?"

"No. I was just bored. I wanted to liven things up."

Phil raised his eyebrows. "You did that, all right. Bramble could have broken a leg."

"I know that. I'm sorry."

He shrugged, and she went on. "The phone calls..."

"What phone calls?" asked Tom.

"That's why she kept disappearing at odd moments," I explained. "Camilla knew."

"I wanted Camilla to think I had a boyfriend," said Georgie, miserably. "I thought that way she wouldn't feel so pleased with herself about Tom."

Tom looked completely baffled. Camilla gave her twin a forgiving hug. "Don't think about that, it was silly. And I'm partly to blame for encouraging you to bring your spare phone." She looked around at all of us. "We thought it'd be fun to break the rules, you know."

We all nodded. We all understood that one.

"Is that the whole story?" asked Tom. "Because I've got this jump-off to do, and to be honest the whole nonsense seems like a lot of fuss about not very much to me."

Camilla and Georgie looked at me with identical pleading blue eyes.

"That's all," I said firmly. "Let's all forgive and forget and just be friends. After all, we're wasting time we could be spending with the ponies."

Tom hurried off to get ready.

I hugged Phil and Megan gratefully but I could see Rosie hovering.

"Jess?" she said.

"What?"

"I didn't realize. I thought..."

"Look, Rosie, I've had enough agonizing for one day. We all know what happened now; it's all out in the open. Like I said, let's just forget about it."

"And be friends?"

I hesitated. Then I said, "Yeah, and be friends," and hurried over to the ring. I didn't look to see if Rosie was following. I didn't really care. We'd never be close friends again, but there were plenty of other people I could trust to be my good friends instead.

Emily was at the back of the crowd waiting to watch Tom's jump-off. We looked at each other in mutual dislike. We didn't speak, and I was glad to see that when Rosie came up, she point-edly avoided Emily.

153

Then we concentrated on what was important – the show.

Tom was in the jump-off with four other riders. They'd all collected some faults, so he had to go clear to win. He took it totally seriously this time, focusing on each fence and keeping Rolo under close control. They scraped the second fence, which was a spread, so that Rolo had to stretch way out to clear it. Then they were clear until they reached the wall – which was a layer higher in this competition. As Rolo soared over it, the near-silence was broken by a sharp clunk as his hoof dislodged a brick. A sigh came up from the crowd. Then Camilla clutched my arm in excitement.

"It's still there, look!"

The brick had somehow stayed in the wall, teetering right on the edge of falling. We watched Tom clear the last fence while at the same time keeping an eye on the brick. You could actually see it swaying. Tom galloped towards the finishing line, and the bell rang. At that very moment the brick finally fell. Would it count? Had he finished on time?

There was a moment of nail-biting tension, and then the loudspeaker crackled into life.

"Clear round!"

He'd done it! We danced around in a circle in absolute joy, all of us, forgetting the dramas we'd been through in a frenzy of excitement. It had been such a fantastic week of trekking and schooling and jumping. All the problems had been worked out. Ahead of us lay a fun evening of barbecue and partying. And Bilbo and Tim and all the other ponies would be there too, just on the other side of the paddock fence, part of everything.

And who knows? Maybe I'd be back again soon!